Wolf A

by Anastasia Drummond

Copyright 2005

*For Rachel who got me started and
Brian who kept me going*

Author's Note

This is a work of fiction.

Mad fiction, I'll be the first to admit. It started its life as a NaNoWriMo novel. After a crazy month of writing the rough draft came months of hard work and ruthless editing. With help and more than a little struggle it has become this.

My thanks to those folks at NaNoWriMo for giving me a chance to try something I'd never have dreamed of doing. Huge thanks to my daughter who challenged me to try it and then help me edit it. Thanks to my husband, who is a good sport about a month of inferior meals in November.

This world you are about to enter exists only in my head. Any resemblance to real places or real people is all part of my imagination. All logical errors and inconsistencies are my fault and are easily resolved as the result of magic.

Thank you for reading my book.

A place of shelter

Struggling against the sea waves breaking over the bow of the small boat, the lone boatman chances a look ahead to try to find a break in the sea cliffs that might offer shelter from the rising wind. The afternoon is starting to fade and the storm is coming upon him from behind. The rising wind is making the sea boil around him like an angry pot. It has to be a fast glance because the tide is pulling and wind is driving the small boat towards the rocks. Only the stubborn, weary struggle with the paddle keeps the small craft from disaster.

A shaft of sunlight breaks through the clouds overhead to show what looks to be a small cove, and the weary boatman increases his efforts to make it to the promise of safety. With a final push through the crest of a wave, the sea slides the small boat into a sheltered bay. Very suddenly the wind drops and the waves become still. A dozen more paddle strokes, towards the centre of the now-quiet water, and he can float quietly and pause a moment to rest. He takes a deep breath, rolls his neck and shoulders and stretches his arms out, holding the paddle tightly as he looks about himself in wonder.

Even to a man totally exhausted by the struggle with the boat, this bay is a miracle to see. It is larger than it looked from the break in the cliff behind him. He can still hear the wind of the storm, noticeably quieter, behind him. He looks over his shoulder to the sea heaving restlessly beyond the edge of the rocks that guard the bay's entry. The bay is in a pocket of sunshine, the sky overhead is clear, the water is still as a summer pond, and the sounds of sea birds echo off the rocks and over the water. Ahead is a band of trees with rolling hills behind them that look like they could be a good place to shelter and rest. He sees no signs of people from a distance, but for the moment that is not as important as getting to shore and resting. The man settles once more into the familiar rhythm of paddling and heads towards the shore.

The boat is a large wooden sea kayak, obviously made by loving hands. There are places where it shows scuffs and scars from encounters with rocks. There are hatches on the front and rear of the craft, covered in treated skins to keep the water out. The man is weathered from being in the sun, and his long, dark brown hair is tied back with a leather band. His brown eyes are surrounded by wrinkles, brought on by the sea, weather and years of thought and travel. His shoulders are broad and strong; his hands well-worked and gentle.

As he paddles towards the trees, he notices that the cliffs on the right are crumbled and softened by many storms, with heaps of fallen boulders. There is a tiny cove, but the hillside in it looks very unstable and not at all a good place to go to shore. He sees that there are small patches of grass in places up the sides, where small, fleet-footed beasts graze. The different colours of stone that have broken away make the beach below look like the front of a jeweler's stall in a market place, offering so many possibilities of treasure.

The left hand cliffs are strange as well, made of sharp cut stone reaching like knives stabbing into the clear sky overhead. Veins of red, pink and green slice through the otherwise grey stone. In some places the stone is broken, making ledges that hang over the water like balconies in a town, each full of squawking sea birds. There are also places where the stone is cut or broken in very regular shapes, rather like intentionally created hide outs. The boatman shakes his head wearily at the fancy his imagination has created from broken stones. The rocks are his friends, they offer him shelter and safety in storm, food from the eggs and birds that live there, and beauty, even when his eyes are so very tired. He turns his sight ahead to the area with trees and continues the steady paddling that brings him closer to the hope of rest and comfort with each stroke.

There is a small forest of mixed trees which grows from the beach halfway up the hill and this is all that he can see ahead. No signs of houses or people on the shore, though further up behind the trees there might be something.

His boat makes fast progress across the still water. After battling the storm, this seems too easy, but he is grateful for the ease of passage and the respite from fighting to hold himself upright against the winds and tide. He also notes that there seem to be two rivers coming into the bay, both curving behind the wall of trees, one on each side. This will give him access to plenty of fresh water as well.

The trees form a thick curtain from the sea, and even with many showing the naked limbs of winter, they are hard to see through. A small pebble beach is just ahead and the boatman slows his craft with skilled strokes and moves carefully sideways to what looks like a reasonable place to land. There seems to be a break in the woods ahead, which offers the chance of shelter and the trees will provide fuel for a warm fire. His belly rumbles in hope of a warm meal. Too many days of cold, sea-soaked meals gives him a deep hunger for fresh cooked food.

There are many rocks just off shore, so he slows and picks his way carefully through them. The ones showing are not so worrying, but their hidden cousins just under the water offer him a chance to be dumped into cold sea water. A chance he has taken too many times, much to the amusement of his companion. He isn't sure enough of the comfort of fire to risk soaking himself any more than he already is.

Finally the ripples ahead show a good place to step out. He paddles the boat in slowly and turns about so that he is facing the sea. Once again he marvels at this bay, sparkling in the sunlight and still as a pond, while beyond the cliffs guarding the entry a storm rages over the greater sea. Even though he can't feel a breath of wind or hear its voice, he knows it is howling madly out there. Shaking his head in wonder, he turns his attentions back to landing his small craft and getting out of it so he can stretch.

He paddles backwards, trusting that nothing will tip him over, feels the keel of the boat ground softly into sand and pebbles. He gives thanks to his gods for a safe landing and frees the edge of the leather deck that protects the inside of the boat from incoming water. Standing up carefully balanced between the sides of the boat, he unfolds his tall body and steps on one foot into the water. It is cold, but not miserably so and only calf deep. He gets his other foot free, still holding the boat and lifts it easily from the water. Even with his gear it is surprisingly light. It is a very sturdy boat, made of strong wood; he spent many hours in the making and building of it.

He carries the boat above the tide line and sets it down carefully, making sure that it is steady on the rocks and in no danger of tipping over. He removes the leather decking from around his waist and lays it carefully over the bow of the boat, to keep it off the ground. The decking will need a rinse in clear water and then to be hung up to dry without cracking. He looks into the main compartment of the boat to see his companion curled up, sleeping. She had been resting on his leg while they travelled. He reaches in to pat her on the head, and without opening her eyes she bites him gently, then goes back to sleep. She will come out later when he has food to offer. She wasn't happy with the rough passage they had just taken and prefers to be left to sleep. For the moment he is fine with leaving her be.

He smiles softly, opens the stern hatch, takes out his pack and fastens it to his back. The boat is easier to carry if he has most of his gear strapped to his back rather than in the boat. Fortunately the inside of the boat compartment is dry, so even if he can't have a fire, there is the promise of dry clothing. Settling the straps in place, he takes another peek at his companion. She opens one eye and blinks at him, then ignores him. He is not bothered by her seeming indifference, as he knows that when he needs her she will be alert and ready to provide advice or defence. Many a night she has stayed awake, keeping watch so that he could rest, so he does not feel the need to give her offence. Besides she tends to bite when she is unhappy and he has enough scars.

He lifts the boat and carries it up from the beach towards the open place in the trees. He wants to explore the area, but has learned that it is better to do it quietly, with his boat out of sight and not risk either hostile folks or giving offence. Between the two open trees there is a glade that is a regular oval shape. Carefully he sets the boat just to the right of the opening and walks around the glade looking for totems or wards that would indicate that it is a forbidden or sacred space not to be used by casual travellers. He finds none and slips his backpack off, setting it carefully on the ground by the boat.

This glade has obviously been used by some traveller before, as there is a place in the back overgrown with soft grasses and moss. It looks like it will be a good place to sleep, sheltered from the wind and out of sight of the opening, but with a view between the trees of the entire bay. Nearby is a ring of stones that has been used as a fire pit, though the fresh grasses growing in it show it has been many seasons since its last use. To one side, grass grows through a stack of dry, broken wood, obviously left for fuel. At each end of the oval is an overgrown path, leading in the general directions of the two rivers. All in all it looks like a safe place to shelter, and with its air of long term abandonment, a place he is unlikely to be disturbed.

He goes back to the boat and opens the bow hatch. From it, he pulls out a pack with bedding and cooking gear and puts it over one shoulder. Walking back to the patch of soft grasses and moss, he shrugs off his pack and sets it gently on the ground. Looking about, he ponders for a moment, trying to decide if he wants fire or water first. Looking over at his boat, he notes salt drying on the leather deck and decides that fresh water is best first. He can pick up more fuel as he walks and get a better idea of the area before announcing his presence with smoke. He takes up his water bag from the main compartment of the boat, noting it is nearly flat, and hangs it from the loop on his belt.

He grasps the decking and holds it in one hand so it drips free of his clothing. He leans down and looks again into the compartment where his companion is still resting. She feels his presence and wakes, stretching with an elegant yawn. He smiles at her and shakes his hair free from its band. He reaches out a hand to her.

"Come, Little One, there is fresh water nearby," he says to her softly, his voice rough from lack of use. "I expect we could both use a wash."

He doesn't have to speak out loud to her, as she is telepathic, but sometimes he misses voices around him. So many years he has been wandering the empty world with only her. He wonders sometimes if he is cursed. Shaking off this negative thought, he lays his hand down flat on the bottom of the boat. She climbs gently up his arm and onto his shoulder, and settles comfortably in the veil of his long hair, her tail curled around his neck.

He strokes her smooth forehead and then sets off down the left path. This one seems to lead towards the hills and his experience tells him if there are folk about, they will be near the hills or in caves. Living out in the open in these times is not always safe. The trees guard the edge of the path and though it shows no signs of recent use, it is still passable. He stops several times to make small piles of fallen branches, to pick up on his return journey. Tonight there will be a warm fire for the two of them.

After a few moments he comes to the edge of a small river, where the path stops at a bend with a small pool. Though the river is fast-flowing, the pool is quiet. There are stones set about the edges that had obviously been used as wash stones, but the moss growing on them show many years of disuse. He looks up the river and sees the place where the trees stop. His curiosity to explore is great, but his need for water is greater. The water he carries is old and stale, so he takes the bag and whispers a prayer of thanks to the water goddess for her gifts to sustain him. then pours it into the river.

He fills the bag with fresh water, ties its neck shut carefully and sets it to the side. He lays down on the ground and puts his whole head into the clean water, scrubs his face with sand and drinks his fill. His companion slips off his shoulder and frolics in the water. She is comfortable in any water, but prefers fresh, especially after so many days at sea. She sends a feeling of happy contentment to him and he smiles fondly at her.

After drinking his fill he stands and wrings out the water from his hair. He knows a bath in the clean water would feel grand, but the day is waning. He first wants to explore a bit, to make sure it is a safe place to rest. He takes the decking of the boat and carefully rinses it off, then lays it across a sunny stone nearby. He stretches himself, squares his shoulders and starts up river to explore.

His companion returns to him and takes up her familiar perch on his left shoulder. She feels his curiosity and though she doesn't share it, she is sure that what he finds is will be interesting. It usually is.

Making camp

He walks along the edge of the river, being careful of his footing on the rounded stones at its edge. There may have been a path up the hill at some point, but the river has changed its course and any path is long gone. The river curves left, away from the sea. Though the trees lead uphill and the opening between them looks close, after several minutes he is still climbing. When he reaches the gap in the trees, he is surprised to find open fields that look as if they have been farmed in recent seasons. He glances around, looking for signs of people, but there appears to be nothing, just empty fields, wild grasses, flowers, and small birds and creatures.

Looking back towards the bay, he is blinded by the reflected sunlight, so he can't see the bottom of the fields very well. The sun will set within the hour, so he wants to go quickly about his exploring. He notes that there is a larger river on the other side of the valley something to go look at in the morning. Again he looks to the bottom of the field, feeling that something is there, but unsure of what he can see. The light and shadows play tricks with his vision.

To his left, uphill, stands the ruin of what looks like an old farm house. The roof is gone and the stone walls show signs of crumbling, with vines growing up the side. There is a wild overgrown kitchen garden that looks as if it may still have something to offer. He passes through an opening in the stone wall, with the remains of a broken gate dangling from a rusty hinge, and walks around the garden, inspecting the plants there. He is delighted to find some late season potatoes and under some leaves, a small, perfect pumpkin. This find makes his companion very cheerful, as it is one of her favourite treats. There are also many familiar cooking herbs. It looks as though their supper will be very filling this evening. The garden is a gift of plenty to a weary traveller and his always-hungry companion.

He walks around the house, to continue his exploring. On closer inspection, he sees that the house has no door or window facing the fields or the sea. All the openings face the forest, and have heavy but broken shutters. He touches the door frame and for a moment melds mentally with his companion. They work quietly together to search for hostile magic or danger. There is nothing here, just small, overlapping memories of laughing children. Puzzling impressions, but there is no malice. This is a relief to the man.

He walks through the door into a large open room and sees a hearth to his left, on the uphill side of the house. Its grate is rusted, as are the holders that once would have held a cooking pot. Along the wall are a sink with a pump, and broken shelves with shattered bits of pottery on the battered wood Obviously this was once the kitchen area.

To his right is open space, with another hearth. There are indents in the floor showing where furniture may have sat, and a bit of tattered spider web like lace flutters at the top of one half shuttered window. This would have been a cozy room, with the fires going. The growing shadows weave odd patterns on the walls, making it hard to make out much more detail.

Ahead of him is another doorway. He walks through and finds himself in a hallway with an opening to either side. A quick look into each shows the remains of what were most likely bedrooms. On the left, again uphill, one room has bunks against the wall, and the floor is scattered with the remains of broken toys. This home shows many signs of children. The room on the right has a large battered and crumbling bed frame in it, obviously the parents's room. The frame of a baby's cradle is beside the larger bed. This was once a family home, but what has happened to the family?

At the end of the hall, on the seaward wall which has no openings, is a niche with an altar in it. It is not unusual for homes to have such things and he wonders which gods once protected this family, or failed to, as the case may be.

He walks towards the altar, feeling something undefined, not unease or worry, but rather a joyful sadness. His companion feels it as well and nudges him on the ear. He pets her absently on the forehead and goes to look closely at the altar. On it is a small stone figure, which he cannot identify in the shadows from the trees and fading daylight. He is reluctant to touch or move it before identifying who it represents. He has learned in his long travels that some gods are jealous of their images.

What interests him most of all is the small bunch of wild flowers at the base of the statue. They look much like something that would be left by a child, as the stems are torn and uneven and they are roughly held together with a long blade of grass. It is a mystery why there are fresh flowers in an abandoned house. He wonders where might the giver of these flowers be? Still there are no feelings of menace, so he decides to return to his camp before darkness leaves him stranded on this hill. He can return again in full daylight and have a closer look around. There might be things left behind that will make his onward journey easier.

He goes outside again and on the uphill side of the house finds a stone shed, with a rusty but serviceable spade in it. He takes the spade to the garden and with some effort digs in the hardened ground to bring up some of the potatoes, carrots and turnips. He sets them aside and harvests the small pumpkin as well. His companion climbs down onto the pumpkin and looks ready to take a bite.

He lifts her up, looking into her beautiful jewelled eyes and says gently, "Little One, I know it is your favourite, but at least let me cook it for you." His voice is cheerful. "Besides, I like it better cooked."

She sends a thought of grudging agreement and curls up again on his shoulder with her tail around his neck. She is asleep in the time it takes for him to take a breath.

He tidies up the ground and whispers a prayer of thanks to the maker of the garden for this feast. He then returns the spade to the stone shed and finds in the corner an large earthenware pot which he takes to carry his vegetables in.

Once again he scans the fields, looking towards the sea. He thinks there might be more houses down there, but the sunlight is still very bright off the water, shining into his eyes, and he is tired. He walks over to the edge of the field, trying for a better vantage point, but the setting sun is a fire on the water and his vision won't clear. He sees stalks of late season unharvested oats at the edge of the field, takes his belt knife in hand and he cuts an armful of the oats down and adds them to his collection of foods. With a little bit of work, he can have hot porridge for breakfast as a bonus. Well satisfied with what he has found and untroubled by hostile magic, he sets off down the hill along the edge of the river.

At the quiet pool, he takes a few moments to wash the vegetables and finds them to be sound and well grown. He put them back in and fills the earthenware pot with water. It is sound and holds water, he is pleased to see. His gods are being generous with their blessings today, and he is grateful. He gathers up a couple of flattish stones and takes them along on the top of his pot. He ties the water flask to his belt and leans down to see that the sun has dried his leather decking nicely. He gathers it up and heads down the path to his camp, feeling more optimistic than he has in some time. He stops along the pathway to gather up the piles of additional fuel, using the leather decking as a carrier sling. He returns to his camp with full hands, ready to make them a comfortable supper.

He sets his burdens down by the fire pit, then walks to the opening in the trees to look out again at the bay. The sun is close to the tops of the cliffs and the sky is turning bright colours. He observes that the storm is still strong at the entry of the bay, adding to the brilliant colours of the sunset.

Has he has lost track of time again? Travelled so long that he has come into the middle to the season of storms, rather than the start, without finding a safe place to shelter? He has been searching for people and so many times just found the ruins where they had been. There are times he wonders if he is all that is left alive. His companion nudges him, sending thoughts of reassurance. She knows he is not the last of his people and that there are other beings as well. He smiles at her and holds her in his arms, petting her forehead gently.

He goes to the fire pit and clears the grasses away, checks the circle of stones to make sure they are in good order. One is broken so he removes it gently and carries it out to the beach. He sets it down and chooses another of the proper size to fill out the circle. He takes some time to clear the grasses from the piled fuel and uses them for tinder. There is a good supply of fuel, so he should have a warm night or two before needing to gather more. Whoever had used this site last had left it in good supply. He would be sure to do the same, in readiness for the next traveller when it was time for him to leave.

From his belt pouch, he takes his fire stones and with practiced ease sets the tinder to light. After a very short time a merry fire burns and his companion curls up on a nearby rock to enjoy the warmth. Setting the flattish stones to the side with the oat stalks, he sets the pot on a flat topped stone by the fire, so that the water in it will boil. He takes the potatoes, carrots and turnips and slices them into small chunks, which he returns to the pot. From his pack he takes some dried meat, herbs, and salt. He cuts the meat into small bites and adds it to the pot as well, except for the occasional piece that gets fed to his companion. He adds the herbs and salt and leaves the pot to boil.

He slices the pumpkin in half and spreads the seeds and pulp on another of the flattish stones from the river and sets it near the fire, but not too close. His companion goes to the pulp and eats the stringy bits like spaghetti noodles, leaving the seeds on the stone. He wants the seeds to dry, not cook, and she isn't interested in the seeds. He takes half of the pumpkin, carefully cuts it into small chunks and put them in the bubbling pot of stew, the other half he sets carefully aside. His companion watches all this closely, but returns to her warm rock to wait for the meal to cook.

The water in the pot starts to boil harder and with a nearby stick he gives the stew a stir. It will take a while to cook, so he turns his attention to the oats. The grain is dry, and with some small effort he manages to get a good pile of oats to pound between his stones. He pours the roughly ground meal into the reserved pumpkin half, adds a bit of water and salt. He then puts the pumpkin in his own battered metal cooking pot and sets it on the back of the fire with stones on top of the open pot and uses other stones to form an oven around the pot, except for the side open to the fire. By morning he should have a fine porridge. Sadly he has no sugar or honey to sweeten it, but it will nourish them just the same.

His supper preparations finished, while waiting for things to cook, he unrolls his bedding. In the middle is a soft blue blanket that he has had for many years. He checks the area of grasses and moss for stones, but it seems to be a comfortable place. He changes his shirt to a dry one and puts his pack and other clothing into the boat, which he turns over. If there is rain in the night, at least his supplies will stay dry. From his waist pouch he takes an old battered spoon, which he dips into his stew to bring up a taste. He brings out a bite of pumpkin and offers it to his companion, she greedily snaps it up. This makes him laugh and offer her another bite, and even though it is not yet cooked to her preferred standard, she doesn't refuse it.

After they have shared out the stew, both feeling comfortably well-fed, he adds fuel to the fire and banks it against his makeshift oven. They will have a hot breakfast as well, a bounty after many a thin day of travelling.

Sitting on his bedroll, looking at the fire, his mood turns thoughtful. Sensing this, his companion curls up in his lap, watching him intently with her jewelled eyes.

"Little One, what do you think of this place?" he inquires silently to her.

She closes her eyes for a moment, reaching out with her mind and then answers him carefully. "Paddler, I feel it is strongly and magically protected." He glares at her obvious answer; sometimes she is very evasive. It is not meanness, just a thoughtfulness in her basic nature.

She avoids his glare and continues, "There are signs of folks here, but some are very old. Yet the fields show recent working, so I expect we will find folks near by. I feel that there is another bonded pair here, quiet, perhaps hidden, perhaps even sleeping." Her brows furrow slightly. "Not really sleeping as much as hiding."

This idea gave him pause, as a bonded pair, he was considered one of the 'others' by folks. Bonded pairs always have and use magic, but their very bonding forces them to answer to the gods and leaves them subject to their wishes and whims. It is not always an easy life.

"Clola, how long have we been together?" he asks her absently, while staring into the fire.

She knows he is in a serious mood, as rarely do they use each other's true name, even in quiet talk. "Kemnay, that is a silly question and you know the answer. I have been with you from the day after you were conceived. Before your birth, I used to rest on your mother's belly and sing to you."

She bites him on the hand gently, trying to break his mood. "Though I remember your mother screamed at me the first time she saw me, especially when I kept trying to sit in her lap. Before she realised she was carrying you, that is." Her mind voice got a little cross. "I was only trying to do my job, after all."

He laughed at this image. Many times his mother and the village wise woman had told him the tale of meeting Clola for the first time.

The Companion arrives

It had been in the early spring and his mother had left the windows of their home open for fresh air. His father had been outside working in the garden and she was sitting at her loom weaving a length of cloth, when suddenly through the window a small green were-dragon appeared. His mother, intent on her cloth, hadn't noticed the creature at first, but suddenly it landed on her lap. His mother had startled and screamed, standing up suddenly and upsetting the loom. The small dragon got dumped off her lap and tangled up in the threads.

At the sound of his wife's scream, his father came running in with a hoe in hand, ready to come to the rescue. However when he got to the door, he caught one end of the hoe on its frame and the other end rapped him sharply on the forehead, knocking him unconscious in the doorway. The young woman continued to scream and the dragon kept trying to free itself from the threads.

The village wise woman happened to be nearby, heard the noise and came running as well. The wise woman was well into her middle years, but quick of motion. Her hair was silver coloured and her eyes a clear blue. She was average of height, slightly plump around the middle. Over her tunic and trousers she wore a coat with pockets everywhere: big pockets on the sides, small ones on the sleeves, and hidden ones inside. She was always ready for whatever life had in store for her.

The scene the wise woman burst in on made her laugh until she had tears running down her face. Here was the young gardener out cold on his own doorstep, and his young wife standing in front of her chair screaming and crying. A small green dragon, looking very annoyed, was all tangled up in threads and parts of loom on the floor. The story had been told in his village many times, much to the embarrassment of his parents.

After a few moments, the wise woman managed to get herself under control, just soon enough to keep the rest of the village outside the gate with a stern command. She checked the young man and found he was not seriously injured, though the large bruised lump on his head would ache for a few days. She set the hoe carefully outside, so he would not do further injury when he woke. The wise woman then went into the house to quiet the hysterical young woman.

The wise woman took hold of the sobbing young woman and set her in the chair with a firm instruction to calm herself. She then turned her attention to the dragon struggling in the mess of threads on the floor.

"Little One," the wise woman said firmly, "I need you to stop your struggling and I will free you from the threads. You have made enough of a mess of that cloth." The small dragon turned a brighter green, then became still and allowed the wise woman to untangle her.

Once freed, Clola again tried to go to the young woman to sit on her lap. She went into a panic and jumped out of her chair. Before the wise woman could grab hold of her, the young woman upset the chair and fell backwards, hitting her head on the floor. She also was unconscious. The small dragon hovered in mid-air, unsure of what to do. The wise woman checked the young woman, found she too was only slightly injured, and left her on the floor. The wise woman held out her arm to the dragon and commanded it to come to her.

Looking into the beautiful, jewelled eyes, the wise woman said sternly, "Listen to me, small spirit of disorder. I realise you have been sent by the gods, but I also realise that they are practical jokers of the highest order. Usually they will send one of you to a wise one first, so that you can be gently introduced. Why have you come directly to this house?"

Clola held on carefully with her claws to the woman's sleeve. The dragon looked at the wise woman and realised she didn't have an answer to the woman's question. She had been linked, by the gods of sky, earth and water, to the soul of the child that had been conceived in the womb of the young woman the night before and sent with all haste to watch over the soul and bond with it. She had been given no instruction as to introducing herself, and told the wise woman this.

Again the wise woman could only laugh, though the underlying seriousness of the situation was not lost to her. It is unusual for a bonding animal to come before the child is known to be well and moving in the womb. This child was to be special, that much was certain. First, she had to calm its parents and get them to accept that they now had another creature to care for in their small home as well as a baby on the way.

"Little one, the villagers here have named me Merry, for as you see I find laughter in most things. This village does not use true names, except among deeply trusted friends and family. Those names are carefully guarded and should be kept so, for strong magic can be used against a creature whose true name is known. So for now you will be called 'Little One,' though I know you are old as rocks and your size is a choice you make, as is your form," the wise woman said seriously.

Clola sent a feeling of pleasure to be recognised for what she was. She said silently to Merry, "I accept your naming of me and understand your warning as well, though I have learned differently. My true name is Clola, I am sent to bond with and protect the boy-child Kemnay." For a moment the little dragon's skin went through a rainbow of colour change.

"Thank you, Clola. I will give you my true name and trust you with it. I know you are sent by the gods for the good of us. My true name is Balmedie, and I am the village wise woman. I see to their healing and ask the gods to grant them favour. This pair was especially favoured by signs for their wedding. Now I am beginning to understand why. Can you tell me more of this boy child, Kemnay?" Merry asked curiously.

Clola said, matter-of-factly, "He will be bonded with me, for all time. He will have strong magic and a clever mind. He will be a traveller when he is grown. The god of sky has given him knowledge to know storm. The earth god has gifted him with the ability to read and have contact with all rocks and stones. The water goddess has offered him a promise that he will never be killed by sea or water, but that should never be told to him, because if he does not honour her, she will do her best to make him miserable without taking his life."

"As she would, if her trust was abused," Merry said knowingly. "These are strong gifts indeed, though I am sad to know he will go away. Do you know if he will return?" For unknown reasons, the wise woman felt a chill down her spine. She was sure that there was more here, hidden by the gods. Such great gifts carried a high price of responsibility.

Clola said, with a shrug that rippled the length of her body, "That is not mine to know. I am sent only to make his magic strong, his wits alert, and to provide protection and teaching."

"Fair enough. What you have told me will give me many things to think about," said Merry seriously. "I am sure we will talk of this many other times, but for the moment we have other problems." The wise woman glanced around the room and shook her head.

Looking to the people laid out on the floor, Merry couldn't help but laugh again. "This is going to be a hard introduction, since you have frightened them so well and thoroughly!"

Clola's scales turned slightly pink, as if she might be embarrassed, though Merry knew that was not the case. Such creatures did not share human sensibilities. Many did not ever learn them.

The wise woman took a few moments and righted the loom, seeing that the cloth threads were in a hopeless tangle. This would not make the young Weaver happy with the new guest, but such things happen in life. Merry set Clola on the kitchen window and offered her a small apple from one of her many pockets. Clola happily munched away, trusting Merry to take care of the folks and smooth the way. The dragon wasn't sure what all the fuss was anyway, but set herself to do what she knew she must.

Merry went to the doorway and knelt down by the young man's face. She pulled a bitter smelling leaf from another of her many pockets and crushed it under his nose. The smell brought him to waking and he began struggling with her. She spoke to him firmly, while holding his shoulder. "Gardener, listen to me. I have news you must hear. Your wife is all right, not to worry."

When he realised it was the wise woman holding him, he stopped his struggle and allowed her to help him sit up. He brought a hand to his head, which was starting to bruise and showing a sizeable lump. He groaned slightly.

"That is going to hurt for a few days, I'm afraid," Merry said gently. "I will make a brew for it a bit later, but you are not seriously damaged." She helped him to stand and held his arm while he steadied himself on the door frame and got his wits about him. He looked over at his beloved bride laid out on the floor and a frown of worry crossed his brow.

"She is alright?" he asked the wise woman, deeply concerned. The young woman was his bride and they had wed only weeks ago. His feelings for her were very strong.

"Yes, of course she is," Merry said with a gentle smile. "However, she too has taken a bump to the head, though not a serious one."

With this the young man looked alarmed and tried to push past the wise woman. "Merry, how did this happen? I must go to her," he said frantically.

The wise woman stood firmly in his path and said, "No, you may not go to her yet. Trust me when I tell you that she is in no danger. First you must listen to what has happened." The young man looked unhappy with this, but accepted her authority without question, while continuing to look at the young woman on the floor.

Merry went on to explain, her voice very soothing and calm. "A small were-dragon flew in the window and frightened your young wife. This small creature means no harm, and in fact she is a protective spirit. However she startled Weaver and got tangled in her threads. Weaver started screaming and tripped over her chair. I have freed the small dragon and spoken with her. She is sitting quietly on the kitchen window, waiting for a proper introduction." Merry pointed in Clola's direction. The small dragon remained still and waiting on the windowsill.

Gardener looked perplexed. "But why has a dragon come into our home? Have we angered the gods? The signs for our wedding were strong." His face was very puzzled.

The wise woman shook her head and realised the young man was rattled from the fright, the rap on the head, and the news. It would take a few moments to let him get things straight in his mind. Meanwhile the entire village had gathered at his gate, and only a strong look from the wise woman kept them from flooding into the house. She could deal with them later, but right now she had to convince these two to accept the dragon -- not that they had a choice. Merry realised

Gardener would not be able to listen to her completely until he was assured that his bride was going to be alright.

The wise woman took him firmly by the arm and lead him over to where the young woman was laying on the floor. When he saw his young wife, he immediately broke free of the older woman's hold and ran to kneel beside his wife. On his knees he cradled her head in his arms, calling softly to her. "Weaver, my beloved. Please wake up." His voice was gentle, but a trace of worry could still be heard.

The young woman's eyes fluttered and she looked up at him confused. "Gardener? Why am I on the floor? I was weaving and then...." Her voice trailed away confused. She lifted a small hand to the back of her head and said, "My head aches."

"Hush, love, not to worry," he said, kissing her face softly. "Do you think you can sit up? Merry is here to talk with us."

"Of course I can sit up," the young woman said. Then she noticed the swelling bruise on her husband's head and said in alarm, "Gardener, what happened to you?"

The young man thought for a moment, but couldn't actually answer. He looked over at Merry who said, "You heard Weaver cry out in distress and came running. However, you forgot to set down your hoe. I believe it caught on the door frame and that is what hit you in the head." The wise woman was smiling broadly.

The young man's face burned bright with embarrassment, but he couldn't think of anything to say that wouldn't sound stupid. Instead, he put his hand behind his young wife's shoulders and eased her up. Then with the gentleness of deep and true love, he got her to her feet, righted her chair and helped her to sit down. He pulled over another chair for Merry and a stool for himself to sit beside his wife.

He held on to Weaver's hand firmly and said, "Merry said that she has something important to tell us, so we must listen now." His head ached and his stomach was a bit upset. The bruise on his forehead was spreading and by the next morning both his eyes would be blackened.

Merry, in the mean time, had gone to the kitchen and filled the kettle, put it on the fire, then made cups of tea for all of them. She added some leaves from another of her many pockets to the tea for the young people, to help their headaches. She took each of them a cup and ordered them to drink. She then went back for her own and sent a silent message to the small dragon to just sit quietly until Merry returned for her. The dragon had finished the apple and with a small burp, curled up on the sunny windowsill and went to sleep. Though the dragon felt strongly she must be close to the young woman, she also understood that Merry was doing her best to help.

Merry pulled the chair around so that her back was to the kitchen window, blocking the view of the sleeping dragon there. She settled and took a sip of her tea. The two young people were looking at her expectantly, so she took a deep breath, collected her thoughts and said, "As you know, the signs for your wedding were strong, the strongest in the village for many seasons. Since you have such a deep love and joy of each other, I had thought the gods were just rewarding that love, but it seems that there is something more involved."

The young man started to interrupt, but fell silent when the wise woman held her hand up. "Last night you conceived a child and the gods have chosen it to be bonded. They have sent its bonded partner and guardian to you."

The young woman blushed at the wise woman's knowledge of what they had been doing the night before. However, the young man looked troubled. In his experience, all too often notice from the gods was not a blessing.

"The child is already bonded? Even before we know of it?" the young man asked worriedly. "Merry, is this right? Doesn't that mean that the child will be cursed?"

Merry set her cup aside on a nearby table and reached out to take each of them by the hand. She spoke in a quiet reassuring voice. "Gardener and Weaver, I trust in the gods that this is good news. Yes, it is unusual for a bonding to take place before the child stirs, but it is not unheard of. No, it is not at all a curse. Do not worry, accept that your child will live and be strong."

Merry decided she would keep the child's sex and name to herself, for the moment, as well as the promised gifts. Some things are better left to their proper time, and right now the wise one needed to settle these folks to the point of being able to accept the dragon.

The young couple exchanged a look, and Gardener leaned over to his young wife and kissed her gently. "Not everyone knows from the day of their child's conception that it will live, be well and guarded. It is good news, my beloved." His eyes shone with true devotion looking at his bride.

Looking into his loving eyes, the young woman returned his kiss. She put a hand to her belly and smiled. "Good news indeed, my love. We will have a house full of happy children, if we can start one so early." Her eyes twinkled.

Merry saw that their love would be stronger than their objections to the dragon. She stood up and walked over to the window. Clola, feeling the presence of the wise woman, stretched and yawned. The small dragon allowed herself to be lifted up by the wise woman and carried over to the young couple.

The wise woman sat again in the chair holding the small dragon on her lap. The young woman frowned slightly and then looked to her loom in tangles behind her. "Oh no, my cloth," she wailed and started to rise from her chair.

Her husband took her hand, restraining her and said, "The cloth can be repaired. I am sure this creature meant no harm." His voice was cheerful. "She is so lovely. I am sure she didn't mean to tangle your threads."

Clola brightened at the man's compliment and sent a thought to Merry. "Tell her I am sorry, that I did not mean to frighten her. I just wanted to be close to the child. I didn't realise what she was doing or that she would respond so loudly." Her mind voice was a bit disgruntled.

Merry smiled, petting the dragon's forehead gently, and said to the young woman, "Weaver, this creature says to tell you she is sorry, she didn't mean to frighten you or mess up your threads."

The young woman accepted this with a sigh. It would take her many long hours to untangle and right the cloth in the loom, but that could not be helped for now. For the moment there were other things to think about, but a small kernel of frustration remained at the dragon's behaviour.

Clola asked Merry to introduce her to them and explain what she needed, keeping the true name of the child secret for now.

Merry lifted the dragon and looked into Clola's jewelled eyes then asked, "Can you not speak directly to them?" Most bonded creatures could speak telepathically with people.

Clola said, "No, of course not. They are dead-end souls. They can't hear me."

Merry took this information with a sad heart, though her face did not change. Many years of carrying secrets had allowed her to keep her heart light, even when it was set to break.

The wise woman smiled, turning the couple and said, "Gardener and Weaver, I would like to introduce Little One. She is a were-dragon, bonded to your child. She will need to be nearby Weaver as much as possible before the child is born and then she will stay with the child for all time. You will be responsible to help feed and care for her, but she will tell me so I can let you know what she needs."

Weaver reached out a cautious hand to Clola and touched her softly. Merry set the dragon in the young woman's lap and left the three of them to get to know each other.

At the gate, the wise woman told the village elders to plan a celebration, as they were to have a bonded child in the village.

Exploring the village

The camp fire has burned down to a pile of embers and the man realises he has been living in the memory of the story of Little One's arrival. It makes him smile and set his mind to ease. He adds a bit more fuel to the fire, banks it, and settles into his bedding. The small dragon curls up on his chest and begins to sing softly to him as he settles to sleep.

After the man has gone to sleep, Little One lifts herself gently off of him. She takes some time to reinforce a protective ward around the edge of the glade, to watch over him while he sleeps. She wants to have a look around on her own. Stepping out to the open beach beyond the trees, she changes form into a great white flying dragon and lifts off over the bay towards the cliff opening. The storm is still raging beyond it.

The bay is very still in the moonlight and the dragon sees signs of fish and other healthy sea life. Skimming down along the top of the water, she grabs a fat fish with an extended claw. She alights gently on a nearby boulder and has a small snack. Shape changing is hungry work, after all. After a moment of preening and cleaning her claws, she is ready to return to her exploring.

At the cliff edge, she hovers, looking out to the increased storm beyond. There is a strong magical barrier here and she is unwilling to try to cross over it. She knows that her bond to Paddler will allow him to always find her, but to try to leave could put them both in danger. That is considered an unreasonable risk by the gods. From the looks of this storm out there, this will be where they will stay for some time.

Once again the season of storms has caught them by surprise. It has gotten longer and more dangerous each cycle, and protected places seem fewer and fewer. People are starting to thin out across the planet, except where they have gathered in safe groups. She knows this is part of the natural cycle of things, but his unchangeable form makes it rather inconvenient. For her, if they are swamped, she just changes, but she can't get big enough to carry both him and his necessary supplies.

The dragon turns back towards the trees and pumps her great wings strongly. As she flies over the trees, she notes the campfire is still burning and Paddler seems to be sleeping quietly. Good, her ward is working well, and he is untroubled by nightmares. At the land ward edge of the trees she hits a magical barrier that will not allow her to pass, she also cannot go to the right edge of the trees towards the larger river. She flies back over the bay, tries to go to the mouth of the larger river and travel up it, but again the barrier turns her. She can fly to the small river, but there she is brought gently to ground. She can walk all the places they have been together, but cannot go any further. Not without him being with her. The dragon reaches out with her senses but is still blocked.

This protective barrier has all the signs of being made and maintained by another bonded pair. The rules from the gods say that a bonded pair can build any protective magic, and they are supreme in that protected area. They cannot destroy or do lasting harm to another bonded pair and any pair can enter and stay, as long as they don't create harm. If the entering pair do harm or intend harm, this offending pair can be held in place or moved outside and forbidden re-entry.

As only half of a bonded team, Little One is stopped from exploring without Paddler. Bonded pairs have strong magic individually, but only together can they approach another protected pair. The great magic requires both working together.

With a shrug, the dragon sends a mental broadcast of peaceful intent, knowing that the other pair will be watching her. She then returns to their camp, shifts back to her smaller shape, curls up next to Paddler's warm body and settles down to sleep. The smell of the cooking pumpkin keeps her awake for a moment, but the snack of the fish will hold her till morning. With a sigh and a yawn she relaxes and begins to snore.

Dawn light filters through the trees and touches the man's face. He blinks and wakes slowly. The dragon wakes also and takes herself over to the rock by the fire, near the cooking pumpkin, hopping comically from foot to foot in impatience.

"Hungry, so hungry," Little One says in mock frantic tones. "I know there is pumpkin."

He looks at her and smiles. "Yes, Little One, I know it is pumpkin, but give me a moment to wake up. I have never let you starve."

He stands and stretches, walks back into the trees where he has dug a privy trench, relieves himself, and returns to the fireside. He notices that the sky overhead and over the bay is clear and the air is mild. Beyond the cliffs, however, there is still evidence of storm. Not a promising sign.

The dragon watches impatiently while he stirs the embers of the fire and adds more fuel. He feels her mood and moves to take the rocks from around his cooking pot. The pot is warm, but not too warm to lift out with bare hands. He uncovers the pot and finds the pumpkin and porridge perfectly cooked. He takes his spoon and bowl and scoops the grain and a small amount of the pumpkin out for his breakfast.

The rest of the pumpkin he sets on the ground in front of her and she attacks it voraciously. He eats his porridge quickly, knowing that if she finishes first he will lose what is left of his breakfast as well.

After she finishes the half pumpkin, skin and all, the small dragon comes and puts her nose in his bowl. She is disappointed to find it empty, though her belly is dragging from being so full.

"Sorry, Little One," he says with a smile, "But I like pumpkin too." He laughs at her greed and rubs her affectionately on the forehead. She flops down with her bulging belly facing the fire and burps contentedly.

The man settles by the fire and relaxes for a few moments, then asks her, "Well, Little One, what did you find when you were out wandering in the night?" Obviously he had felt her leave him in the night, even in his sleep.

"I believe we have delayed until the season of storms," Little One says. "Though it feels too early to me. There is a protective ward at the edges that keeps them out of this area."

Paddler nods at this information, it is as he expected. He had felt something as he crossed over into this bay, but at the time was too busy to look at it carefully.

Still prone on the ground, Little One continues, "I flew over the bay and caught a fine fish, but could not go past the line of trees or any place we had not already been together. There is another bonded pair here."

Again he nods, this fits with his overall impressions as well. "How strange that they have not approached us, then. Nor do there seem to be many signs of other people. It is unusual for bonded pairs to be out alone. Unless they are, like the two of us, on a search," he said to her, tossing more sticks on the fire. "I suppose we shall have to go looking for them."

"I suppose we will." Clola says with a burp.

He looks at her bloated form by the fire. "Perhaps when you have managed to digest that pumpkin enough to actually move, that is," he teases. "I think you are getting fat."

Insulted, the dragon sits up indignantly and bites him on the arm, drawing a small bead of blood. "I am never fat," she says, sounding annoyed.

"That wasn't nice, you cat," he says, laughing at her. She hisses at him warningly and makes as if to bite him again. He puts himself out of reach and says apologetically, "I'm sorry, Little One, I know you are not a cat." His twinkling eyes have more teasing in them as he continues, "A goat, perhaps, but never anything as elegant as a cat."

She shifts into her great white dragon form, which crowds the glade, and says threateningly, "I could bite your head off if I wanted to."

He reaches up and pats her forehead, saying seriously, "Yes, I know you could, but you won't. Come on now, let's explore the other path. I believe we can do it if we are together."

She gives up her irritation, shifts back into her smaller, green form, takes flight and lands hard on his left shoulder. He pretends to stagger under her weight and she pulls out a mouthful of hair. "Truce, Little One," he says consolingly. "I was only teasing. I'm sorry I called you names."

Mollified, she decides to go to sleep, curls her tail around his neck and burps again. It was a very good pumpkin, and she hopes they will find more of them. As is her habit, she falls instantly asleep.

He takes a few moments to tidy up his camp and bank the fire so that there is no danger to the surrounding trees. He does not want to be kicked out of a safe place because of carelessness with his fire. Satisfied that all is in order, he walks down the right-hand path.

This path is longer than the one he had followed the night before and darker under the trees as well. It seems to wander slowly, then opens out at the mouth of the river. The man sees that it is a much larger river than the other. Turning to walk up river, he sees more trees. He carefully makes his way through them and is surprised to suddenly find himself on the outskirts of what had been a fairly large village.

At the river's edge are the ruins of a stone pier, with a few rotted timbers along it. There are some shreds of rope and below the water he can see remains of boats. From the size of the pier, it looks as if it could have handled ocean-going ships as well as local fishers. This had once been a lively harbour, from the looks of the buildings in shambles nearby, but it seems as if it had been left in a hurry. Most fisher-folk would not just leave a boat to sink and rot.

Turning towards the main part of the village, he sees many stone buildings, but none have their roof intact. Some still have storm shutters, and there is even an occasional intact door. He walks into a nearby building and surmises from the debris left inside it that it had once been a pub. He closes his eyes and lets his mind open to the feelings remaining there. He feels and hears layers of laughter and happy companionship, talk of fishes and wives and fish wives. This had been a gathering place for the men. He smiles sadly at the loss of such a merry place. How he would like to have joined the company for an ale!

Leaving this building, he walks among the remains of what had to have been shops. Some had upper floors, and the floors below have more remaining in them. He is careful not to actually move anything, as he is only exploring and looking for some answers. Until he finds the local bonded pair and settles with them, he wants to be sure to give no offence.

Off the main street he finds homes. He looks into them and notices that each shows a niche with an altar. He now expects that these are in honour of the protective pair and again leaves them undisturbed. He has never felt the need for such trappings, but other folks have other ways.

However, in many of the homes by the hearth there seem to be piles of white stones. These give him an uneasy feeling, so he does not go near them yet. He did not remember noticing if there were any in the house he had visited the night before, but the shadows of sunset would have hidden them anyway.

Uphill towards the fields, there are more trees. In them he finds a magic circle whose interior is carefully and lovingly groomed. He again does not enter; this he will do later if he is allowed to. Clola stirs slightly as he gets near it, but doesn't fully wake.

There is something that this town needs from him. A deep sadness that requires attention. However, until he can get a few more answers, he must wait to act. His companion agrees silently with him, in a sleepy way and increases her ward around them to protect from unexpected attack.

He walks around the magic circle to the left, sun wise, and goes to the line of trees. There, as he expects, he finds a path leading uphill towards the fields. It is a close and very dark path, even in the bright light of day. It curves around between the trees, but always continues in an uphill direction. Carefully, he walks along it, all senses alert.

When he comes out of the trees, he is at the bottom of the fields and a statue stands in front of him. It is obviously old, but shows no sign of weathering. Around the base are many different kinds of beautiful wild flowers, all brightly in bloom, as if it were summer instead of the onset of winter. There is a strong feeling of magic around it, though no menace, just a loving and protective magic. This would be the centre of the ward of protection around the bay and perhaps the entire isle. The bonded pair were near, or at least had been recently.

He walks around the base at a reasonable distance, looking closely at the statue. The figure on the square base was very unusual. The stone seems to be white marble from the neck down, a small, female humanoid form with wings, rather like the myth he had heard of angels when he was a child. However the head is black granite in the shape of a wolf. A very startling combination of creatures which makes little sense.

Looking up to the face of the statue, he says out loud, "I am a traveller, in need of shelter. I ask that my companion and I be given leave to remain until it is safe for us to continue our journey." Bowing his head, he adds, "I offer whatever poor services we can give to aid your protection of this place."

For several minutes, the only reply he hears is the wind whispering through the trees. He begins to wonder if his senses were wrong about the statue being linked to the bonded pair. However, Clola reassures him that this is the source of all the magic in the area. She indicates he should just wait, so he stands silently looking at the beautifully odd statue.

A strong wave of grief overcomes the two of them, bringing tears to the man's eyes and nearly knocking him over. The powerful emotion hits them like waves on the shore and just as suddenly stops. A small thin female voice says, "Stay as you wish to, do what you can, but do no harm. We will not interfere with the healing you offer." He feels the source of the voice close itself away from him and he tries once more to reach it.

"Wait," he calls out, "Please tell me what happened? How I can help?" There was nothing but the feeling of magic and silence.

Perplexed, he asks his companion, "Little One, did you hear more that I missed?"

She shakes her head negatively. "No, Paddler, just an injunction to heal."

"But heal what?" He wonders what has happened in this place to drive the bonded pair into grieving silence.

He whispers a prayer of blessing to this unnamed pair and a plea to his gods for assistance. This task is going to be very difficult, especially with so little information to go on. He doesn't expect an answer, as more often than not his gods will leave him to struggle his way through a situation as a lesson. He accepts the plea and the task the pair have given him and turns back to the path to the village. He is sure that at least some of the answers are there, though in his heart he dreads what he may find.

He avoids the magic circle, as for now it cannot be of help to the search they are on. It is probably part of the solution, but for the moment if offers more questions than answers. He is also not sure the bonded pair here will let him enter such a place without resistance.

He walks into the nearest home, goes to the niche in the back wall and lifts the carving there. It is of the Wolf Angel, so at least he knows the source of protection, even without the details. He gently returns the icon to its place and whispers a prayer to his gods.

With a deep breath, he walks over to the hearth stones and sits on the floor. He looks at the grate, at the wall behind and finally with a heavy heart at the white stones piled there. With a shaking hand he reaches out to this small pile of white stones and lifts them into his hands. Cradling them near his heart he has a shock as he starts to understand part of the problem here. These stones, these pure white, innocent-looking stones are sitting in nearly every building, all over this village.

Dead-end souls. He has come into a village full of dead-end souls.

Paddler's memories of the past overwhelm him and he lowers his head and weeps as if his heart will break.

Panic

When the tragic event happened, he was a man of over five and thirty storm seasons old. He had worked with Merry for a long time and she was ageing, telling him her time was nearly through. He was not worried because he had seen the cycle of life and death all his few years. He thought he understood why souls needed the constant cycle of birth, death and rebirth. The one thing he didn't understand was dead-end souls, souls that had no hope of rebirth. His parents were such a pair, but they were very happy people, who loved life well. Merry didn't have any good answers for him. It made her both happy and sad to know the dead-end souls, but because her own teaching had been broken, she didn't have the answers he needed.

He had been their only child, but they were well and truly satisfied with him. Their home was a peaceful place, and once his mother had accepted Clola's presence in the house, it had become a very happy place, often filled with laughter. Clola learned to avoid Weaver's threads and loom. Weaver learned to keep the dragon well fed. When Gardener found out her love for all things growing, especially pumpkins, he grew great crops of them. He was a gardener of unmatched skill, so the dragon always had a good supply of very beautiful and tasty pumpkins to satisfy her.

Early in his childhood, Paddler developed a love for boats and water and was soon apprenticed to Boddam, who was the village's master boat builder. The builder was a dead-end soul, loved in the village for his jolly laugh and skill in his craft. He was always willing to lend a hand where needed. He could make the fastest and strongest boats, and even mend the boats that had been run up on the rocks and looked hopeless. It was believed by many that the gods had given him special magic. Far and wide folks would come to him for water craft, advice or just a friendly visit. He was always willing to stop, have a pint of ale and listen when needed.

Boddam was a large, strong man, with dark hair and sun-darkened skin that gave him an exotic look. In his twinkling eyes the joy in life always shone through. He was unmarried, though the ladies seemed to like him, and without children, so when Paddler started to visit him, in his workshop, the boat builder naturally would talk about his craft and show the small hands how to handle the tools. The two were fast friends and soon Paddler's skill with the tools was only slightly less than Boddam's own, which made the old man smile with great pride.

Boddam also loved Little One. He would often laugh at her antics and send her out fishing for them. In this way he taught Paddler that the dragon was not only a playmate, but a helper as well. Little One would often sit on the bow of Boddam's boat and shift her weight, just to see if she could dump him in the sea. Occasionally she managed it, but just as often he would anticipate her and dump her in first by making a quick turn. It was a game often played, much to the laughter of all.

While they worked together, Boddam would often tell Paddler of his travels as a young man. He had spent many years on the sea, exploring the isles of the world before finding this village to settle in. The trees here were good and the seasons reasonable. There were enough rocks to keep the sea interesting, but not so many as to be a constant risk to life and limb. He showed the younger man the special boat he had built for his travels and taught him how it was made. Paddler built one to match and soon they could be found out on the sea playing amongst the waves, or disappearing for days to explore local isles. Boddam taught him not only boat building but what was needed to travel between the isle: how to make a fire, find food or shelter, how to live in the wild places. Skills that had held the young man in good stead since he learned them. Beyond the purely practical knowledge, the old man shared his love of the world as well.

After many years of happy association, including sharing the rooms at the boat workshop, Boddam died. His death was celebrated by the village, because his life had been such a gift. Paddler stayed in the workshop to finish the projects that had been left behind, and started new boats when they were needed as well. Many expected Paddler to take the old man's place as the village's master boat builder, but he was already hearing the call of other places in his heart. The stories Boddam had told him as a young child teased his imagination, but for a time he was content to take over the old man's place and mend boats. He would know when the time was right to travel, this he was sure of.

Paddler would often take his special boat and go out among the rocks, and occasionally on an overnight trip to a nearby isle. He was curious as to why there were so few folks on the isles nearby, though there were signs of them, things left behind and abandoned. He spent time practising turns and rolls, so that he was not often surprised by what the waters could do to him. He had deep respect for the sea and the sea goddess and always gave her his thanks when he was safe back to shore. His deep love for the sea was obvious to any who spoke to him. He became familiar with most of the sea creatures, knew which could be approached and which were best left alone, as well as which would make a good supper. Clola was always willing to help him with that.

Seasons passed and his parents aged, as did Merry. Folks in the village kept waiting for Paddler to look for a wife. There were several young women in the village who would have been happy to live with the little dragon in exchange for a clever and talented husband, though the dragon would often show how difficult she could be by starting an argument in public. She frequently tripped the young man or knocked him out of chairs. The inn keeper gave him only wooden mugs, because she so hated the smell of ale she would find ways to break the pottery ones. The dragon was not and would never be easy to live with. Paddler was also considered handsome, though he never seemed to be aware of that in himself. If there was a perfect woman for him, she had not yet come into his sight, at least that he had noticed.

One night, after he had spent a long day working on a new boat and coming to a place he had to wait, he found himself hungry and not willing to cook his own food. He considered going down to the inn for a meal, but thought his mother would be willing to feed him. Little One thought this was a good idea since it was pumpkin season, and the chances of getting a meal of pumpkin were very high. This decided the issue, because he knew giving her her way would assure a peaceful nights sleep. Besides, his mother was a better cook than the inn keeper. Together they walked up to his parents's house.

At the gate Paddler paused and thought about all the times he had spent there. Growing up among the plants and the threads, watching his parents' deep love for each other. After he moved out, his mother often would leave food in the rooms attached to the boat workshop for him. She never said anything about his moving away, but he always knew she was thinking of him. He knew she accepted his growing and was glad of it, but he would always be the child of her heart.

His father would often walk down for a visit and just happen to have a bag or basket of produce from the garden for them. It was less often of late, as his father seemed to be moving noticeably slower nowadays.

Mostly his parents were very happy in their love for each other and had more than enough for their now-grown son and his voracious companion.

He walked up to the door and rapped on it. Of course, before he had pulled back his hand his mother shouted for him to come in, that dinner was on the table. He smiled at how well she knew him. He walked in and found her setting hot food on the table and saw a baking dish by the hearth that looked like it had a very large pumpkin in it.

Clola was about to launch herself off his shoulder to go after it when his mother looked at them sternly and ordered, "Don't be in such a hurry, Little One. First you must wash. You are covered in sawdust and varnish and it won't be good mixed with the food." Her voice was stern, though her eyes sparkled. Little One checked her attempt at flight, knowing she could wait a few moments.

Paddler kissed his mother on the cheek and went to the sink to wash. Little One slid off his shoulder and under the water from the pump, then sat on the edge of the sink draining her scales. She knew better than to wander around the house wet. That might get her chased away from the wonderful pumpkin, a risk she wouldn't take.

As much as Weaver had accepted the dragon, she was not above chasing after her with the broom if she felt the creature was not behaving well. Weaver was the only person who could seem to get Little One to behave. Paddler would try reasoning or ordering and sometimes fighting with the dragon to try to get her to do what he wanted. His mother needed only to give her a stern look and the creature would check her behaviour. He often wondered if he should borrow his mother's broom on occasion and try using it to work the dragon's stubbornness out. Clola heard this idea in his mind and bit him on the arm, out of sight of his mother, who objected to the dragon chewing on her son.

After the two of them were clean and dried off, Paddler carried Little One over to the fire and set her beside the baking dish. It was a full pumpkin, with meat and other vegetables baked inside. The dragon growled softly and thrust her face in the food. Gardener joined his wife and son at the table and after wishing them a good meal, they all ate with gusto. This was the one place Paddler could relax with his food, as he knew the little dragon would be too content to try and eat his meal as well. His mother would be unhappy to know how much her son had to fight his companion for food when they were out of her sight.

While they were eating, Weaver paused and looked up at Paddler, asking, "Son, when are you going to find a wife? I should like to know that you will be well taken care of when it is time for me to pass from this life." She had said this to him many times in his life, so he never took it very seriously. He smiled at her and winked at his father, who stayed out of this discussion.

"Mother, I am perfectly able to take care of myself. You taught me very well," the young man replied, reaching for more bread. "Don't worry so much. There are many years to think of such things." He helped himself to another plate of food, glancing over to make sure the dragon was still content. Her dish was empty and she was laying with her belly towards the fire, burping softly. "Besides," he said, pointing, "what woman is going to be willing to put up with that bad-mannered creature?"

Little One burped contentedly at him and stuck out her tongue, thus proving his point. The three folks around the table laughed at her and went back to their meal. The dragon's manners, or lack thereof, were a source of amusement to most of the village. Weaver had heard stories, but could never get her son to own up to them, and dismissed them as just gossip. Paddler managed to change the subject to the boat he was building and then asked his mother about what she was weaving. She got caught up in the distraction and was telling him about the types of threads and colours she was using to make a new blanket for him.

After the meal, when the dishes had been cleared, the family sat around the main hearth, talking softly. Weaver moved her loom close to her chair and showed him the nearly-finished blanket. It was soft, with many shades of blue as a background and had the pattern of a small green dragon who looked to be swimming in water. It was a beautiful, magical bit of work that would keep him warm and feeling loved for many a night. Paddler protested that he had many good blankets, but she waved his protest away. "You never know when a spare will be handy," she admonished Settling herself in her chair, she pulled the loom close so that she could work as they talked.

Little One waddled over and peered around the edge of the frame, being very careful not to touch it. Weaver sent her an unnecessary warning glance to keep her distance, though the dragon had only once made a mess of the threads in the loom, Weaver had a long memory and was unwilling to give the small creature another chance. It had taken her more than a week to straighten out the threads and repair the damage to the loom after that. She accepted Little One in her life and accepted her son's need for such a companion, but she hadn't forgotten or forgiven the dragon for that first horrid mess of her threads. Little One knew this and kept her distance, but she was always curious about the loom and the magic of its contents. She did turn to Paddler and say to him, "Tell her thank you from me. It is very beautiful."

Paddler relayed the message to his mother who reached out and patted Little One on the forehead, with a smile. She did accept the dragon and this made it easier. Besides, his mother appreciated folks enjoying her work and knew that not only her son would benefit from the warmth of the blanket. It made her feel good to know she could help give comfort to her son's protector as well.

His mother picked up her shuttles, closed her eyes and whispered a quiet prayer before sending them across the threads. So great was her skill that even in conversation with the men, not a stitch was missed or dropped. The last few inches of the blanket seemed to grow like magic. Clola, fascinated by the moving shuttles, watched for a while, but then decided she was sleepy and wandered over to Paddler, who lifted her up and held her to his chest while he talked with his father about the ideas he had for changes in the garden down at the workshop. The dragon relaxed to sleep, held close. The older man's eyes shone from the paleness of his face. Gardening was his second love, after his wife and family. He was a grateful and happy man. Plants were his gift and he was always happy to share that gift, even just in the talking about them.

That night though, Gardener was feeling very tired and his chest was tight. He was sure it was only from the digging that he had done earlier in the day. He had been working with his compost heap and it was heavy work. He was also feeling very short of breath. He mentioned with a slight laugh to Paddler that he was starting to feeling his age. Weaver looked up from her loom,
concerned. "Perhaps you should go to bed early, my love," she said encouragingly She thought his face looked pale and he seemed to be

sweating. A frown of worry crossed her forehead, and for a moment her shuttles paused on the loom.

Paddler was also starting to notice that his father was not looking very well and he stood to get a glass of water for him. He shifted the dragon under one arm as he walked towards the sink. Suddenly his father cried out in pain, clutching his chest, and he fell from his chair to the floor. Weaver leaped out of her chair, knocking over the loom and ran to her husband. Kneeling on the floor, she cradled his head in her arms, calling to him. His eyes were closed and the pain on his face was great. Tears ran down her face as she turned to her son and begged, "Kemnay, please help."

Kemnay was startled to hear his mother speak his true name, something that was so rarely used, on top of the shock of seeing his father fall. He thrust Clola into his tunic, went over to his parents and reached out to hold them both in his arms. The agony in his father's face was dreadful to see, as was the fear in his mother's. He didn't know what to do, but he was sure he had to do something.

Gardener's eyes fluttered. He took a breath, looked up at Weaver and whispered, "My beloved wife, it looks as if I shall go on before you. I promise I will wait for you. I love you." His eyes fluttered again and his breathing became ragged, though the pain on his face seemed to ease slightly.

Weaver frantically cried out to him, "No, don't go without me. Please, my love, don't leave me to be here without you. Don't go into the darkness alone." She was rocking him in her arms.

She turned her streaming eyes to her son. "Please, Kemnay, do anything, don't let us be separated. I'm afraid we won't find each other again." The pain in her face was greater than his father's. The young man began to feel panic.

Paddler's first thought was that he wanted to go running for Merry, sure that she would be able to help. However, he could feel his father slipping away and the pain in his mother's eyes was overwhelming. Without realising what he was doing he grasped the two of them in his arms and in total panic made a demand of the gods.

"Do not let them be separated! I will not let them be alone without each other," he cried out desperately. He felt the power of the gods attend to his call, not realising how they would answer. Clola tried to pull away from him, but before she could, it was too late.

Stones and consequences

In the moment before his father's last breath, when his mother had leaned down to kiss her beloved husband's face, suddenly they were gone. In their place were two white stones, joined together, sitting on the hearth quietly. Paddler was astonished and frightened. He didn't touch them and looked frantically around the room for his parents.

He grabbed the dragon from his tunic and stared into her eyes. "Clola," he screamed in alarm, "where are they? What has happened?" He continued to looking around the room and at the stones, but he was afraid to touch them. He was very near hysterical with panic.

Clola, knowing that he would need more calming and help than she could give at the moment, ordered, "Kemnay, we must go get Merry, right this moment, even if you must carry her back here. Quickly, we must go now!" The man didn't hesitate. He went dashing out, leaving the door ajar and ran, yelling, towards the wise woman's home. Folks in the village came to their windows, alarmed at the noise he made. Little One flew over his head and landed on the ground near Merry's door.

Merry was dozing in her chair in front of the fire when she felt something happen. It was a feeling that something had moved in the universe that should have been left alone. Then she heard Paddler's cries and told her apprentice Achath to fetch her shawl and her stick. She was standing by her door when the distraught young man burst through it.

"Please, Merry, I need your help," Paddler cried. "Can you come?" His eyes were roaming the room wildly. Achath reached to touch him in comfort, but he flung her hand away. The young woman stepped back, turning her face so he could not see the hurt in her eyes. "Merry, it is terrible, please." He grabbed the old woman by the arm and tried to pull her with him.

Merry touched his hand and he released her. She walked slowly over to the doorway and said, "Yes, Paddler, I will come, though if you are in a hurry, you must needs carry me unless Little One would be willing.

She seems calmer than you are and is less likely to drop me." He didn't appear to be listening, and he was all but pushing her out of the door.

When the old woman got out to the gate, she turned to the dragon and asked, "Little One, can you please carry me? I will aid you with my magic." The dragon shifted to her great white form, gently took the woman in a claw and took flight over the rooftops.

Though the wise woman had never been carried by the dragon before, she had no fear of falling. She knew Clola would guard her well. Her own magic made her light enough for the dragon to carry easily. She had intentionally left the young man behind. She wanted to get ahead of Paddler, who she could see running below, so that she could ask a few questions of his companion before his panic stirred things up.

Little One landed softly in the front garden of the house and set Merry down gently. She flapped her great wings to help prevent the curious neighbours from coming in the gate. Merry held up her hand and told them to wait outside the gate for now, but to allow Paddler to pass when he arrived. Clola shifted to her smaller size and went into the house, telling Merry to follow her.

When Merry walked into the house, she could feel a change, but could not identify what had happened. "Little One," the wise woman asked, "where are Weaver and Gardener?" The dragon moved over to the hearth and indicated the joined stones with a claw, being careful not to touch them.

"Balmedie, they are here," the dragon said quickly. "Gardener was dying and Weaver called to her son to keep them together. He panicked and reached out to the gods. Because his emotion was so strong and he had hold of me, the gods have allowed them to be turned to stone, but they will always be together. Sadly, they are trapped here instead of going on as they should have."

The dragon glanced at the door and said urgently, "We must get them moved to the village circle and blessed, tonight, the sooner the better. We must calm Kemnay's panic, otherwise, what he has caused to happened will spread and it will be disaster for all of you. Kemnay must be the only one to touch them. If you can get him to move them and bless them, it will be all right, for all but them." The dragon looked sad. "They are together for all time, as they wished, but this will disrupt the wheel. The gods will want much for what they have done this night." The dragon looked very thoughtful.

Merry was sure the dragon was right about the gods demand for payment. She understood that she had to act quickly, but getting Paddler to co-operate was not going to be easy. There was a commotion at the gate, and an instant later Paddler burst through the door, once again searching the room for his parents.

The wise woman lifted her hand to stop him: she pointed to his father's chair and he obediently sank into it. Looking confused, he asked, "Merry, can you help? I seem to have lost my parents." He looked so like a lost child rather than the grown man that he was. She was moved with memories of this young man, but knew time was short. She had to reach into him, past his grief and guilt, to do what needed to be done. She took the dragon's warnings very seriously.

Merry walked deliberately over to the overturned loom and carefully set it upright. There was a tangle in it, but the last stitch had been made, as she touched it the blanket came away from the loom and into her hand. Weaver's final gift for her son had been finished. The wise woman held the soft blanket to her face and for a moment felt her own tears behind her eyes. Weaver and Gardener were good friends and she would miss them. Telling herself sternly that she could cry later, she took the blanket over and wrapped it around the shoulders of the young man sitting by the fire. He pulled it around him like a hug from his mother, which is exactly what it was intended to be.

The wise woman pulled over Weaver's chair, took the dragon up from the floor and put her gently in Paddler's lap. He cuddled the creature from long habit and Little One began to sing softly and soothingly to him. Balmedie took his hands in hers and looked into his eyes. Speaking quietly, she told him, "Kemnay, your parents are gone. I am not sure how you called the gods to you or how you caused it to happen, but you have melded their souls to each other and taken them out of the circle of rebirth. Though in truth," she added, "I believe they were already out of the cycle. You have turned them to stone and trapped them in this place." She pointed to the joined stones sitting on the hearth.

He looked at the stones and turned his stricken face to the wise woman. "Oh no, Merry," he begged, "please tell me how to get them back." His eyes burned her heart and she felt her own tears start to slip out.

"I cannot, child," she answered as gently as she could. "This is beyond my skill and knowledge. I only know we must move them to the village circle right away."

She wiped her eyes with the corner of her shawl. Reaching down, she tried to lift the stones from the hearth. She wanted to see if she might read them, but her hands would not touch them. The magic around them was beyond her skill. She turned to him and said, "They must be moved to the village circle tonight so that they can be protected and so that what has happened won't spread." The wise woman touched his hand again. "You will have to carry them, child, as it is beyond my powers to touch them." Quiet tears slipped down her face, knowing she could not even say good-bye to the souls of her friends, only mourn them.

He looked at her, aghast. "But Merry, this is their home, they are happiest here. I don't want to take them from here." He shook his head wildly in refusal.

Clola sat up and bumped him firmly on the forehead and told him a half truth. His panic had to be calmed before it could do more damage. "Kemnay, if you do not move them, now, tonight, the gods will take every soul in this village and do the same to them. Your parents are together. That is what they wanted, but they would be unhappy with you if you let this happen to others that they loved. Take them to the circle now," she ordered, bumping him harder on the head.

He hesitated, then gave in and reached down to the hearth. For a moment he was too afraid to touch the stones, but finally he gathered his courage and lifted them reverently into his hand. They were a warm, welcome presence in his hand. Because he could read stones, he felt his parents and their love for each other. He also felt their love for him and their thanks to him. Holding the stones to his chest, he put his head in his other hand and started to weep.

Clola could feel the energy building in his grief and knew she had to break through to him. She leaped off his lap and shifted to near his size, then took him by the scruff of the neck and shook him like a rag doll. The sudden attack startled the young man and he immediately tried to reach up and get her to free him. This broke the contact of the stones from his chest and he hung on to them as hard as he could, still trying to get the dragon to let him go.

"Little One, that hurts," he yelled. "Let me go!" With his feet off the floor he had no leverage to make the dragon release him. In that instant, his grief was broken through and he was able to collect his thoughts. He looked at Merry with hopeless eyes, asking, "You are sure this must be done now?"

Merry looked at Clola who nodded, shaking the man again. "Yes, child and it must be done now. Let us go together." She started walking towards the door. As she reached it, she called out to the folks gathered at the gate: "Assemble everyone at the circle, and bring torches. Quickly now." The folks hurried to do her bidding, but there were many dark and frightened looks sent back to the house.

Clola carried Paddler to the door and released him outside, out of sight of the hearth. She took the blanket from his shoulders and walked back to set it on Weaver's chair. For a moment she nuzzled the soft fabric and felt a spear of grief in her chest. In her own way, the dragon had loved the woman as well. She moved rapidly out of the door and shifted so that when she landed on the man's shoulder, she didn't knock him over.

Paddler held the stones in a closed fist to his chest and walked resolutely down to the place in the village where there was a magic circle. One of the village men lifted Merry up and carried her so she could keep pace with the young man. At the circle Paddler hesitated for a moment, looking at all of the flowers around the stones. These had been lovingly planted and tended by his father and the sight of them kept the tears flowing down his face. Around the outside of the circle were all of the villagers, young and old, holding torches, waiting for the wise woman.

Merry stepped within the magic circle and beckoned him to follow her. He hesitated for a moment, his hands tightening over the stones, until the dragon on his shoulder bit him quite hard on the ear to get him moving. He swatted half-heartedly at her, but stepped into the protection of the magic. As soon as he crossed into the circle the feeling of dread was lifted from the villagers and they all turned to listen to Merry speak to them.

Merry closed her eyes for a moment, feeling the passing of something terrible that had missed them by the smallest of spaces. She sent a prayer of thanks to the gods and looked at the people waiting silently around her.

"My dear friends, family, and all within the sound of my voice. Tonight Gardener and Weaver have left us, and have left the wheel of birth and rebirth, but they are forever joined together. We will leave them in this safe place, where Gardener's flowers will always watch over them. Our sorrow at their loss is small compared to their joy in each other and their son." She indicated Paddler standing before her. "He asked the gods for help, and this was the answer. They will never be separated." Her voice flowed like water over them all.

A small murmur of distress rippled through the people outside the circle. Merry knew she must calm their fears as well or Paddler, even with the protection of the dragon and the grace of the gods, would become unwelcome in the village. It was not time for him to leave, despite this mischief.

Merry continued, her voice reassuring, "Gardener was dying in great pain, and his wife called out to her son to help. He has helped them the only way he could. Because we have them here, because we honour their love for each other and all of us, there will be no danger to the rest of the village, of this I am sure." Again she felt a ripple in the crowd, but this time it was of reassurance and acceptance. She went on, "They are happy now, together always, but they will be grieved by all of us, and most of all by their beloved son. Let us hold him to our hearts, as we always have, and honour the gift of their lives."

Many faces turned to the young man standing silently and crying before them, and the wave of compassion was enough to shift him for just a moment. He looked out to the familiar faces around him and was surprised to see smiles when he had expected only anger. Once again, as she had so many times in his life, Merry had smoothed the way for him.

The wise woman beckoned him to come forward and he did so. At the base of the largest stone was a bright red rose bush that bloomed no matter what the season. It was one of many plants in the village that had been Gardener's pride and joy.

Merry said to him, "This is where they should rest together. Set the stones in the ground here."

He looked at her, his naked grief making her close her eyes for just a moment. She could no longer stop her own tears, and they flowed freely down her face. "Yes, child, you must," she said to his unspoken question. "There is no choice now. It is our final gift to them. They will be safe here." He nodded silently, unable to speak around his own tears.

Kneeling, he reached out and scraped a small hole at the base of the beautiful rose bush. For a moment he held the stones to him and felt his parents' love one last time, then he set the stones in the hole. He carefully reached up to pick one of the flowers from the blooming bush to put with them. A thorn pierced his skin and a drop of his blood fell on the stones as he laid the rose in the hole. He whispered a prayer of thanks for their lives and their love for him. He covered the stone and the flower with earth, then stood with his head down, eyes closed, begging the gods to make this all a terrible dream and to let him wake from it. Wishing like he had never wished for anything in his life.

When he opened his eyes, nothing had changed. He still stood before the stone, and knew the small disturbed place below the bush was all that was left of his family. Merry reached out her hand to him and he took it gently. Turning, she walked with him to the opening of the circle. For a moment she felt him resist leaving, but her insistent hand pulled him into the arms of the people of his village, many who wept with him and rejoiced in the memory of his parents. Many hands touched him in comfort, many lips kissed him in compassion and many voices shared their deep love for him and each other. Despite himself, he was comforted by their kindness.

They led him back to the inn and put a pint of ale into his hand. He was settled into a comfortable chair by the fire, with the dragon on his shoulder. The folks gathered around him, speaking their memories of his parents. Many wore cloth that had come from his mother's loom; others spoke of the magic his father had with all plants, how there had been no hunger when he designed the gardens for any home's kitchen. Merry stayed close by his side, bringing him back to them with an occasional touch. He did not remember much of what was said to him that night, but he remembered the comfort given.

Later, the wise woman's apprentice Achath came and convinced the old woman to retire to her home and her bed. The young man sat by the innkeeper's fire, even after all the villagers are gone to their homes, until it burned down to nothing and dawn was coming between the curtains at the windows. The dragon occasionally shifted her weight on his shoulder, so that he was aware of her.

He finally stood, setting his untouched mug on an empty table nearby, and walked out of the inn to his workshop. He knew he would have to return to his parents' home and do all the things that must happen when folks were gone, but for the moment he couldn't face it. He had never felt so tired in all his life and didn't know what to do now. Clola told him matter-of-factly that the best thing he could do was feed her and get some sleep. He decided to let her fish for her own breakfast and at least try to sleep. For once she decided to let him have his way without a fight. Though she was not as upset by the night's work as he was, she too felt the relief of a narrowly averted disaster. She would be watching to make sure the village was safe and out of the gods' hearing, but for now he didn't need to worry about such things.

The dragon jumped down from his shoulder, shifted to her great white form, and set off over the sea. For a moment he watched her leave him, but his mind was so numb with shock and exhaustion that he couldn't even send a thought to follow her. He walked into his room, not bothering to close the door behind him, fell upon his bed fully clothed and succumbed to sleep. A while later, after feeding herself well, Clola flew in an open window and settled next to him. She noticed the open door, but was not worried about it. She knew they would be in no danger and it was not so cold that having the door ajar would be a concern.

Dark thoughts by the fire

Kemnay weeps over the memory of his loss, as he sits on the floor of the ruined house clutching the stones to his chest. He will not listen to the voice of the dragon trying to reach him.

The depth of his emotion disturbs Clola and she nudges him with her forehead, trying to break through his feelings. When he does not respond to her nudging, she shifts herself slightly bigger and nudges harder. He eventually falls over from her nudging and she manages to get hold of the hand with the stones in it. With deft claws and a few nips on his fingers, she gets him to release the stones. They clatter to the floor. With their release he starts to get himself under control.

While he wipes his eyes and catches his breath, she shifts back to her small form, carefully gathers the stones and returns them to the hearth where they had come from. She would be just as happy to take them out and drop them in the sea, but knows this would only make his distress return in greater measure. She also knows she has to get him away from this place and back to the fire. He needs food and time to accept the task ahead, and besides, she is hungry again as well. After all, it was only half of a rather small pumpkin for breakfast.

He looks at the stones and the pain in his eyes is a terrible thing to see. He makes as if to take them up in his hands again, but she shifts larger and trips him so he falls backwards and ends up flat on the floor, looking up through the roofless home into the open sky.

She shifts back to her smaller size and jumps onto his chest. She looks into his eyes and says with a whine, "Paddler, I'm hungry. Is there another pumpkin?" She hops impatiently on his ribs.

Usually this would make him laugh, but now it only brings a quiet look to his face. He nods at her, acknowledging her request and struggles to stand, holding her close with one arm. It is an awkward process, and she does nothing to help make it easier. He eventually gains his feet. Intentionally not looking towards the stones by the hearth, he holds her close and goes outside the house. With determination born of desperation he sets her on her usual place on his left shoulder, then strides briskly through the village to the forest path. In a short time he is back within her protective ward, sitting at the fire, and feeding it pensively.

He makes no moves towards feeding himself and more importantly, her. She knows all that is in their camp is dried travel food, so she decides to take matters into her own claws. She goes out to the bay and shifts to a large blue water form and dives into the sea. Wandering about in the shallows, she spies several crabs, and scoops up as many as she can carry back to camp. She drops them into the pot he had picked up the day before. She returns for more, stopping to eat one raw. So lovely and crunchy.

When she gets back the second time, she finds the crabs escaping the pot and he is still just staring at the fire, so she drops a nice lively one on his lap. The crab, as is natural for it, grabs hold with a claw and gets a fold of cloth covered skin on the tender bit of the man's leg. This startles him out of his funk and leaves him jumping around comically trying to dislodge the crab as he finally realises what she has done.

"Ouch, that hurts!" Paddler bellows. "Why in the name of the sea goddess are you dropping crabs on me?" He has finally managed to get the crab to let go of his leg and he is rubbing the tender spot with the other hand.

"I'm hungry," Little One said levelly. "Besides, I only dropped one on you."

"So eat. There are enough crabs here to satisfy even your endless belly," he says crossly, glaring at her.

"I want them cooked," she says with a pout and settles down in a circle, moving the escaping crabs inside it. They can't hurt her scales and she will sit there until he gives way and does what she wants. He knows that once she has made up her mind about something she will not be moved.

"Honestly, Little One, you are so spoiled," he says as he picks up the now-empty pot.

Stubbornly, she remains herding the crabs on the ground and says haughtily, "I am not spoiled. We have a deal. If I catch food, you have to cook it. I have caught lunch, so get to work. I'm hungry."

Children

In the camp by the sea, Clola awakes suddenly. She feels him sleeping and is pleased, but she is also aware of two other people in the area. She decides she had best go up to where he is resting and keep watch over him. She flies up and sees him in the sunshine, notes that he has found another pumpkin, and is pleased. She settles on the corner of the garden wall so that she has a view of the valley, him and the trees behind. She stretches out on the sun-warmed stones and lets her colour change to match. At a glance, she looks just like another stone in the wall except for her jewelled eyes, which when open sparkle in the sun.

From behind the house comes the laughter of children. This perplexes Clola. It is unusual to find folks anywhere near places where dead-end souls are, as they are considered unlucky. She wonders where the children are from and how many other people might be nearby.

Suddenly from around the house come two children, twins by the look of them. Both are dressed in tunics and trousers, with sandals on their feet, and each carries a bag over a shoulder. One has long blonde hair, haphazardly held in a bright ribbon, and the other has shorter blonde hair. They seem to be about seven storm seasons old.

They stop for a moment in the sunlight, allowing their eyes to adjust and come directly over to where she is on the wall. Once again she is surprised, usually she is unnoticed until Paddler introduces her or if she is countering a threat. There is no threat from these children, only a deep sense of wonder. "Just children, nothing to worry about," the dragon says to herself.

"Oh look, I told you there was someone here," the girl-child says excitedly. "Isn't she pretty!" She reaches out a hand as if to touch Clola, but the boy-child grabs her hand. Clola just waits to see what will happen, happy for the moment to just observe.

"Ythsie," the boy child says, scolding, "You know it isn't polite to just touch others without introducing yourself first." He frowns at her and releases her hand. "You know as well as I do what mama says about being polite."

"Oh Skene, I am sure she doesn't mind, she said we were nothing to worry about," the girl-child says brightly. Turning to Clola, she asks, "Do you mind, if I pet you? You are so lovely."

Clola is astonished that not only can they see her, but they can hear her as well. "It is best to introduce yourself first, actually. I am called Little One." She sits up on the wall and allows herself to change back to her normal green colour. She bows slightly, which makes the young girl-child laugh brightly.

The girl-child smiles with delight. "Oh, you can be different too, how wonderful," she says cheerfully. "I'm Ythsie and this is my brother Skene. We live in the village over the hill." She points randomly towards the woods behind the house.

Clola sends a feeling of pleasure to the small pair and says quietly, "I am please to meet you, Ythsie and Skene, and of course you may touch me, if you are gentle." The small dragon stretches out her neck towards the children.

Ythsie puts out her small, grubby hand and runs it over Clola's warm scales. "Oh, you feel so lovely. All warm from the sun and smooth!" Ythsie exclaims. "Smooth like beach stones and your eyes look like jewels." She sees her brother is holding back, looking a bit concerned. "Skene, don't be afraid, she won't hurt you." Looking to Clola, the girl asks, "Will you, you beautiful thing?" The child continues to stroke the little dragon, who gives a mental purr of contentment.

Clola looks at Skene and sends another wave of reassurance. "As long as you are gentle and don't hurt me, I have no need to hurt you."

Ythsie teases her brother slightly. "Little One, don't be offended. My brother is a bit of a 'fraidy cat."

"I am not," insists Skene. He is unwilling to be teased by his sister, so reaches out his small hand to the dragon. Clola notes that it is quite clean. An interesting pair, these two, but she is always happy to be with folks that appreciate her. Clola puts her forehead under his hand and shows him how she likes to be stroked. In a few moments the children are laughing loudly. The dragon looks over at her companion and sees that he is still sleeping peacefully, so draws no attention to him.

The children settle into the warm grass and the dragon hops down from the wall to sit near them. Ythsie starts digging in her bag -- it has a normal assortment of child treasures in it -- and she brings out two sandwiches wrapped carefully in cloth. Skene unhooks a water bag from his waist, reaches into his bag and pulls out some carrots and fruit.

"Would you like to share our picnic, Little One?" Ythsie asks politely as she sets out a torn off bit of sandwich in front of the dragon.

"Please do," Skene says, offering her some of the carrots and a small apple as well. They share out the modest feast and have a merry picnic in the sunshine.

Clola burps contentedly and Ythsie giggles. Skene gets up and says, "I am going to wash in the river. Come on, Ythsie, you are a mess." The children race to the edge of the small river and splash about in the water. Clola cannot resist and flies over to join the fun.

The man half wakes, thinking he is hearing the sound of children laughing, a sound that has to be in his dreams. He has not seen anyone alive for more seasons than he wishes to count. He can't honestly remember the last time he heard a child laugh... but it feels so real.

Sitting against the wall, he rubs a rough hand over his face. Waking fully, he realises he still hears the laughter. Suddenly through the gateway in the wall come two small children with Clola. A look of total surprise crosses his face, followed by a smile. The man stands up slowly.

Skene notices the man first and grabs his sister and tries to push her behind his back.

Ythsie turns to Clola and demands loudly, "Who is that?"

Clola flies over to him and settles on his shoulder. "This is my friend Paddler, we travel together," the dragon answers. "Don't worry, he won't hurt you."

To the man she says, "Paddler, meet my new friends. Ythsie and her brother Skene. They shared their lunch with me." Clola burps lightly.

Silently, he says, "Lucky you, you little goat." She bites him on the ear gently. To the children he says politely, his voice gravelly with disuse. "I greet you, Ythsie and Skene. It is always good to meet new friends. I hope Little One left you some of your lunch." He offers his hand in a peaceful gesture and Skene steps forward and takes it gravely.

"Hello, Paddler," the young boy says in a serious child voice. "I have another half of a sandwich and some carrots left, would you like them?" His young face is so serious it makes Paddler's heart ache a little.

"Thank you, Skene, that would be very nice," Paddler answers with a smile.

Sitting down on the ground beside him the children give him the remains of their lunch, which he eats gratefully. It has been long years since he had fresh bread. Travelling has its downsides, at times. Clola continues to sit with the children and let them pet and admire her. For a change, he is allowed to eat in peace.

Skene looks at the sun and says, "Ythsie, it is time to go back. We've chores to do before dark." The boy turns to the man and asks in his serious way, "Would you like to come see our village? Our mother runs the inn and always has a spare bed for someone travelling."

Paddler looks at him and nods. "Yes, I should like that very much." He lifts Clola to his shoulder and stands.

The children look up at him in wonder. "You are very tall," says Ythsie, with a mischievous grin. "I'll bet you can see forever from up there."

He smiles down at the girl-child and responds lightly, "Not quite forever, but just far enough."

Ythsie giggles, then digs into her bag again and comes up with a small packet. "I have some sweets here. Would you like one? They aren't anything special, just some candied pumpkin," she says offering one up to him.

Clola begins to hop on his shoulder and makes as if to fly at the child, he puts up a hand and stops her. "Wait, Little One, there is no need to scare this child with your greed," he says silently. The dragon settles alertly, with her claws digging into his chest.

He accepts the treat and says to Ythsie, "Thank you, Ythsie. I hope you don't mind if I give mine to Little One. Pumpkin is her favourite thing and we have not had sweets in a long time." He holds the candy just out of reach of the dragon's stretching neck.

Ythsie nods and looks very pleased as Clola takes the treat in one claw and begins to chew on it. "That's okay. I wasn't sure dragons liked pumpkin. I have another that you can have." She holds the piece up in her small hand for him.

"That is very kind, thank you. I like pumpkin too," he says, quickly putting the offered piece into his mouth quickly before Clola can get hold of it. She bites him on the ear, only half-heartedly, then returns to chewing on her prize.

The candy is a wonderful sweetness that brings back memories of other times for him.

The two children go racing around the house to the low place in the wall. He follows, his long strides managing to easily keep up with them. The laughter he has shared with them has cheered him greatly, and he is looking forward to actually having folks to talk to, as well as sleeping in a real bed.

At the top of the hill the children race over, when he is suddenly brought to a stop. There is a magical barrier here and he is unable to cross it, even with Clola working with him.

After a few moments, Ythsie returns to find him moving sideways with his hands out along the edge of the hill.

"Come on," Ythsie says impatiently, "It is this way." She points towards the top of the hill.

Paddler looks over to her and says quietly, "I'm sorry, Ythsie. I would like to. However, I can't seem to come any further."

"Oh that's right, you are a grown up so the magic stopped you. I'll run down and get Balgavney, she'll know what to do. Wait here," Ythsie says in a rush as she disappears over the hill again.

He settles himself on a nearby boulder and waits patiently. For whatever reason, the guardians of the valley are not yet ready to let him go over this hill to the village beyond.

The Wise Woman

After a short time he hears Ythsie's giggly chatter and an adult voice. He stands and walks as close to the barrier as he can. Over the top of the hill comes Ythsie, leading a middle-aged woman by the hand. The woman is tall, with a long braid of hair the colour of copper fire. Her long skirt is a dark green and she wears a tunic of light brown. Over one shoulder she carries a satchel with many pockets. From her belt swing many pouches. She smiles at the child patiently. When she looks up at him, her crystal green eyes shine brightly. She has a kind face, with small wrinkles on it brought about by loving joy and much laughter.

Ythsie is speaking swiftly, her words tumbling like water over stones. "Here he is, Balgavney. See, I told you I found someone. And just look at his beautiful little dragon, she can change colour and everything." The child is breathless in her explanations.

The woman comes to a stop and lifts her hand to the child, who quiets. In a strong, musical voice she asks, "Ythsie, introduce me to your friends and then return home. You are late for your chores and your mother will be cross."

Ythsie looks hopefully up at her. "But Balgavney, I thought you might want me to stay here and help you talk to them," she says, poking the dirt with one sandaled foot.

Balgavney gives her a stern look and says, "I am sure I will be able to talk to them without your help. Now introduce us and begone, child, for it is not my backside that shall feel the stroke of your mother's hand."

Ythsie rubs her backside in memory and says quickly, "Balgavney, this is Paddler and his dragon, Little One." She points and then says, "This is Balgavney, the wise lady," then in a running whirl of dust the child is gone over the hill.

Balgavney looks after her for a moment, laughing softly. "I greet you, Paddler and Little One. It has been long years since we have had others to visit. I had begun to think there were none left."

"I greet you, Balgavney," he says seriously, with a bow of respect to her wisdom. "There are others and regular folks as well, though their places in the world grow fewer and smaller each season. I am a traveller and have just barely escaped the season of storms by coming into this bay." He looks back over his shoulder "I have set a camp in the trees below and was exploring. I have spoken, only briefly, with your guardians who seem willing to allow us to stay, but I can not seem to cross over this hill."

Through his explanation the wise woman nods, but with the last finally looks surprised. "You actually spoke with them?" she says in wonder.

Paddler is puzzled by her surprise. "Well, I'm not so sure I can say I spoke with them so much as received a cry for help from them. I did not see them, except for the statue in the meadow below."

Balgavney nods. "That would make more sense. You are the first to even hear them in a very long time."

"Why?" he inquires, his brow creased in confusion "Don't you speak to them often? I would think as the local wise woman you would be in close contact." The man felt this situation getting more complicated all the time.

Balgavney looks at him with a sad smile. "I can see there is much that needs to be explained to you," she says with a tired sigh, "but first I must speak with the village elders about this and you. We need to discuss what it may mean to us, before we try and explain to you."

The wise woman straightens her shoulders as if coming to grips with a problem within herself. "I would like you to understand, I can no more go into the valley than you can come over the hill right now. Only a few people can cross the barrier and only to certain areas. The farmers can go to their fields, the children to the old farm, but none of us can go beyond the trees or down the rivers, into the village or near the statue."

He looks at her and opens his mouth, with so many questions ready to burst out. She holds up her hand to him, as she had done with the girl-child Ythsie. He takes a breath and accepts for now his questions have to stay within himself. "Please, be patient," she requests. "Are you two willing to meet me here tomorrow morning? An hour after sunrise would be good."

"Of course," Paddler replies, calmly. "After we have had breakfast."

"Thank you for your understanding and compassion," the wise woman says softly. "I dearly wish that I could greet you properly and take you to the village, to be among our people. You have an air of being too long alone." She reaches her hand palm outward in a gesture of friendship, towards the magical barrier. Her manner and bearing remind him of Merry's apprentice Achath.

He is humbled by her kindness and her perception. After just the few moments of talking to her, there has awaked a deep hunger in him for the company of other people and makes his loneliness so much harder to bear. He reaches his hand towards her, also palm out. Though they can not actually touch, he can feel her gentle welcome and he returns it wholeheartedly with a smile.

Suddenly, approaching voices interrupt their quiet moment. Over the top of the hill come Skene and Ythsie, pulling a middle-aged woman by the hand. The woman has the same blonde-coloured hair as the children. She wears an apron over her long blue skirt and lovely red tunic. Though she is obviously hard-working, there is a joy in her face that is reflected by the children. She is a good, sturdy farm wife and has a heavy basket over one arm.

"Look mama, see, I told you," Ythsie says excitedly. "There is a dragon and isn't she beautiful." She points to Clola, who is sitting on Paddler's shoulder.

Skene, not to be left out, says excitedly, "See mama, he is tall enough to see forever." He points to Paddler.

The woman smiles kindly at the children and says firmly, "Hush now, wee ones. Let me have a word with Balgavney without having to over shout you."

The children quiet, though they fidget beside the woman. She sets the basket down beside her.

"Balgavney, these two came back with stories of giants and dragons. I had thought they were playing games to get out of trouble for coming in late from their playing, but after listening to them, I realised that we must have a traveller," the woman says calmly.

"Indeed we do, Tifty," Balgavney says quietly, with one of her brilliant smiles.

"Well then, I doubt the Wolf Angel will let him cross the hill, so I expect he will be happy for some fresh food," the woman says. "I've made up a basket of a few things."

Turning to her children, she orders, "Introduce me to your friends now, so we can give them supper." The children smile.

Skene walks over in front of Paddler and speaks with his serious politeness. "This is Paddler and his friend Little One." The young boy points to each as he speaks.

Ythsie, not to be left out, interrupts and says, "This is our mama and she has a basket of things for you."

Balgavney adds softly with a smile, "Her name is Tifty. She is mother to the twins."

Paddler can't help but laugh at the enthusiasm of the children and he is deeply touched by the kindness these people have already given him. "Truly there is no need, dear lady," he says courteously. "I have found some vegetables in the garden below, we have travel food, and Little One is a good fisher when she wants to be."

"Oh, nonsense," Tifty says sternly. "I've no doubt you have food, but no comforts." Turning to the children she motions to the basket between them. "You two carry this over to them and be careful with it. I'll not have you spilling the milk pot."

The two children each put a hand to the basket handle, carefully carry it over to Paddler, and set it by his feet. Little One leans off his shoulder with her claws in the front of his tunic, trying to climb down him get a look into the basket.

Ythsie sneaks a glance over one shoulder at her mother and digs into her pocket. She holds a hand up to Clola, with another piece of sweet pumpkin on it. Clola quickly takes it and bumps the child gently, forehead to forehead, in thanks. Ythsie giggles and returns to her mother. Skene reaches quietly for Paddler's hand and slides a piece into his palm as well. Once again, Paddler is touched by the kindness of these good people. He slips the sweet into his pocket.

"Many thanks to you, Tifty, Ythsie and Skene. I am sure this will make our supper a much grander meal," Paddler says quietly

"Enjoy it, and know you are welcome here," Tifty orders. She turns back to the children and states, "Now, you rapscallions, there are chores to do. Scoot on home." She takes each of the children by the hand and hurries them down the hill, but not without a wave of farewell from the two young ones.

Balgavney stands watching after the retreating trio with a smile on her beautiful face. She pushes her hair back over her shoulder and smiles at Paddler as well.

Paddler returns the wave to the children and says seriously to the wise woman, "Balgavney, thank you as well. I look forward to seeing you tomorrow. Now, I expect it is best for us to make our way down the hill before the sunset."

Balgavney turns her brilliant green eyes on him and smiles. "If I know Tifty, you will have enough for supper and breakfast as well. Thank you for accepting her gifts."

"When it is so freely and lovingly offered, how can I refuse?" he says with a smile. "Besides, you have no idea how much this creature will eat if I let her -- there may not even be enough for me to share," he says, pointing at Clola, who is still contentedly chewing her sweet. He has hidden his in his pocket for later, though he has no doubt she knows it is there.

Clola bumps him rather hard on the side of the face and Balgavney laughs. "Such a tiny wee creature as that, I am sure she doesn't eat more than a mouse." Clola beams at her.

"You must have very big and hungry mice around here," Paddler says, laughing.

The wise woman laughs as she walks away. "Until tomorrow morning. Enjoy your supper and rest well."

"Rest well, lovely woman," he whispers to her retreating figure.

A welcome meal

He leans down, grasps the basket handle firmly, and lifts it up. There is a clean towel over the top of it, but the smells coming from it make his stomach rumble with anticipation. Clola settles on his shoulder and burps from her treat. She is more than ready for more food, but knows he will share. The sooner they get back to camp, the sooner she can explore the wonderful smells coming from the basket.

The man walks down the path and steps over the wall. He takes a moment to see that he has left everything tidy, then goes to the gate opening and picks up the pot. What a surprising day it has been -- and it isn't even dark yet, though the sun is starting to set.

He stops at the river to wash the vegetables he has harvested and fills the pot with water. He takes a moment to refill the water skin as well, tying the neck tightly. Lifting up his burdens again, he walks back to his camp in much happier spirits than he had left it.

He sits by the fire, adds fuel to it, then uncovers the basket. Clola pokes her nose in one side, and he gently pushes her away. "Give me a moment, Little One. I am sure there is plenty for both of us."

"Hurry up," the dragon says impatiently. "I could starve in the time it takes you to do things."

"Unlikely," the man says with a laugh. He starts going through the basket.

On the top of the basket, wrapped in another towel, is a still-steaming pie in an earthenware dish. It smells of beef, onions, and vegetables as well as many good herbs. He wraps it again for a moment and digs deeper. There is a small dish of blackberries next to the milk pot, which has a lovely layer of cream floating on the top -- perfect for the berries. Below that is a loaf of fresh-made bread, a slab of butter and a small pot of jam, as well as a package of sweet cakes and a tightly corked jug that turns out to be strong ale when he opens it. There is also a small joint of beef, also cooked in wonderful herbs. A layer of straw separates the bottom of the basket where he finds a pouch of porridge grain, four fresh eggs, a slab of bacon and a small pouch of sugar. This last obviously meant for their breakfast.

A truly rich gift. He pauses for a moment to whisper a prayer of thanks to his gods for the kindness of the woman Tifty and her children. He hopes it is not their supper he has been given.

He takes his battered cup and files it with the strong ale. Clola smells it and backs away hissing, which makes him laugh. He takes the milk pot and carefully scoops the cream onto the berries and sets the rest down for her to drink. She laps it up happily while he has a sip of the ale.

Paddler takes the beef joint and sets it down for her and lifts the pie out for himself. She will be happy with either, or both if he would let her, but he knows she is in no danger of starving. Given the chance, though, she might let him go hungry. She chews on the meat hungrily while he enjoys the warm pie. After he eats about half of it, he sets it on the side of him that is away from her and reaches for the bread. With his belt knife he slices off two large chunks and smears them with butter and jam. One he sets down for her and the other he takes a bite of for himself. The bread is freshly baked and he makes a happy sound as he continues his meal.

After he finishes the pie and bread, and pours himself another cup of the strong ale. Clola has shifted slightly larger so that she can crunch the bones of the beef joint more easily. They have not been this well-fed in a long time. After a short while he takes up the bowl of berries and cream and offers her a sweet cake, which she takes happily. They finish their meal, both feeling comfortable and welcome.

"Not bad, for a meal with no pumpkin," the dragon says with a burp. "Remember to remind her I like pumpkins so the next basket will be better." She flops down beside the fire, with her bulging belly sticking out.

"I will make no such request. I have a pumpkin that we can have for breakfast," he says, pointing to the pot sitting beside them. "Do you want it boiled or baked?"

"Baked, whole," the dragon says after a moments thought.

"Seeds and all?" he asks with a raised eyebrow. "So you think not to share and I don't get to make porridge in it this time."

"No, I don't want to share. I only got the tiniest bit this morning, after you took out your porridge," she says, sounding like she is pouting.

The man laughs and knows that to argue with her is a waste of time. Even if he could feed her pumpkins twelve times a day, she would never feel she had enough.

He takes the whole pumpkin and sets it in his metal pot, builds up the stones around it again and banks the fire. The eggs and bacon will be a fine breakfast for him, so he doesn't mind not sharing the pumpkin. He packs the rest of the bread, butter and jam back in the basket and covers it with the towel. He will wash the other dishes in the morning before he returns it. Taking the jug, he pours the last of the strong ale into his cup and relaxes, pondering the day he has had. He realises he is very tired from all that has happened and needs to sleep.

Paddler thinks about the statue and the strange whispered cry for help. Why won't the pair show themselves or speak openly with him? The feeling of grief returns, but brings questions instead of tears to him this night. He shuts his mind to the grief and takes another drink from his cup.

With a renewed sense of times past, he becomes aware that he is looking forward to meeting Balgavney in the morning. He realises with a start that she has given him her true name, as had the others, without hesitation. It is the first time he has ever come to a place and been greeted by people using their true names. He remembers Merry telling him over and over that to use a true name was to invite danger, yet these people showed no concern at all when giving theirs to him, a total stranger.

The mysteries of this place just get deeper and deeper the more that he finds. Why are these people still near the village full of dead-end souls? Why does the barrier limit where they can go, but at the same time so obviously protect them from worry? The type and quantity of the foods he had been given point to a comfortable life of plenty. Why did the children bring flowers to an altar in an abandoned house? Why do they play there at all? Why can they see Clola when she is in a hiding form and talk with her openly?

Why is the village full of dead-end souls and why did their protector turn them all to stone? From the look of things, it happened suddenly and the village was abandoned quickly. It seems that their protector had done it to themselves as well, changing into in the form of the statue. How could they have done that?

This makes him remember his own village and the pain of that memory makes him shake. How he wishes he could learn to turn himself, or at least his heart, to stone.

Clola looks up at him and says, "You didn't know that would happen. You panicked. You didn't know why it should or shouldn't happen. There was no one to teach you. Merry did what she could, but there is only so much a wise woman can do." The dragon's voice is compassionate but firm. "The reason we are travelling is to find the way to change the fate of your village, or to give you enough time to learn to accept life it as it is."

Paddler nods to her, but his throat too tight to speak. Never could he accept what he had done. He takes another drink of the strong ale and forces his thoughts back to this place. He knows he will have to face himself, but that makes him afraid and after such a day with so many changes of emotions, he does not feel he has the strength. This place and these people need his help, but he is unsure where to start. Taking a moment, he whispers another plea to his gods for help, not expecting any answer from the silence of the trees.

The man finishes his cup and rinses it out. He lifts the vegetables out of the pot, setting them on the top of the clean towel. No reason to have to wash them again. He pours the porridge grain from the pouch into the water in the pot. He stirs the mix then sets it on a rock by the fire, to let it cook slowly during the night. He takes a few moments to relieve himself at his privy trench and returns to his bedroll. After he settles, his companion crawls over to him and stretches out on his chest, begins to sing softly to him as they both drift off to sleep.

Meeting Balgavney again

At dawn the sunlight wakes him, shining into his eyes. Clola is snuggled beside him in the bedroll and he moves carefully so as not to disturb her. Going to the fire, he stirs the embers up and adds more fuel. The porridge smells good and he stirs that as well. Taking a few moments to go off to his privy trench, he stretches his legs and walks out to look at the bay. As always, the bay is still and quiet up to the point of the cliff edges, and then the sea is a mass of teeming white caps. The protection here is absolute and they are safe -- confused, but safe.

Walking back to camp, he picks up a few more dead tree limbs for fuel. Since he is going to stay, he needs to work to get more fuel. He wonders about taking over the old farm house up the hill and staying there. He will have to ask Balgavney if that would be acceptable. He will also have to be careful of the dead-end souls there. He is sure he could remake the roof with a few borrowed tools. He wonders if any of the people of the other valley can come across the magic barrier to help him.

Back at camp, he sets down his fuel by the fire and starts moving the rocks from around the pumpkin. He feels Clola under his elbow and looks down at her. She is hopping from one foot to the other in impatience. He stops for a moment with the rocks and strokes her forehead; she bites his hand and nudges him back towards the pumpkin.

"That wasn't nice," he says rubbing his hand.

"I am starving," she says as she frets, "and you are being slow. Hurry up!" She nudges his elbow again.

Laughing, he gives up arguing with her and continues to take the rocks away. When he gets to the metal pot, he dumps the pumpkin out on the ground and steps back as she attacks it. It is nearly half her current size, so it is going to take her a while to demolish it.

He takes the warm pot and sets it back near the fire, then gets the bacon and eggs out of the basket. With his belt knife he cuts the bacon into chunks and then throws them into the pot. After a few moments the smell of cooking bacon fills the glade and he stirs the cooking meat with his battered spoon. When it is ready, he breaks the eggs and scrambles them in with the bacon. In a short time it is cooked and he takes the pot off to the side on a nearby rock. He watches the small green dragon with her pumpkin while he eats his own meal. She has gotten through the top and has her head inside. She pulls her head out to look over at him for a moment, her face smeared with cooked pumpkin strings and seeds. He laughs again and digs into his own breakfast. She ignores his laughter and goes back to her meal with relish.

When he has finished the meat and eggs, he goes to the pot and finds that the porridge is perfectly cooked. He takes a bit of the butter and some of the sugar, stirring both in carefully. He sets the pot off to the side to cool for a few moments while he makes a cup of tea. With his belt knife he cuts the remaining bread in half, splits the butter and jam between the slices, and set hers beside the nearly demolished pumpkin. He relaxes back with his own bread, porridge and tea, and watches her finish her meal. Once again she is bloated with food and laying with her belly facing the fire, burping. He reaches down to stroke her gently. He is feeling much more optimistic after a second night of comfortable sleep and several decent, fresh meals.

"Clola, it looks as if we shall be staying here for a while," he says softly while he strokes her full belly.

She rolls her jewelled eyes at his obvious statement, too bloated to bite him. "Well, the food is good enough," she says happily.

"It is that," he says, looking at her with a wicked grin. "But I can see I shall have to start watching you more closely -- you eat too fast and too much. I am sure you'll soon be too fat to carry."

The little dragon hisses at him again, but burps and ruins the pretend menace. She has enjoyed her meal too much to be very aggressive, even to his teasing.

Leaving her sprawled out by the fire, he gathers up the dishes and pots, taking them down to the seaside. He scrubs them with sand and piles them together. He will rinse them in the fresh water of the river before going up the hill. He is mindful of the kindness given in these dishes and is unwilling to return them less than perfectly clean. He returns to

"I am sorry as well," he says, looking at her seriously. "I would not be the cause of tears to anyone, especially a beautiful woman." Something about this woman reminds him so of Achath, making his heart sad.

A ghost of a smile crosses her face briefly, and she whispers, "Thank you," and blushes, the colour making her face even more brilliant. The wise woman looks off to the distance, reluctant to start telling her story to this strange but handsome man sitting near her. She has many questions about him as well.

He sees her hesitation and decides an indirect question may be best to get her talking. He says nonchalantly, "I am surprised to find you use your true names here. This is the first place in all my travels I have found that to be so. Do you not fear having magic used to hurt you?"

She snaps back from the memory she was drifting in and laughs in surprise "Of course we use true names! A person cannot be hurt by using their name against them. That is one of the laws of the old gods that got twisted by unlucky traders. I am in no danger from my name being known and neither are you." She smiles quietly. "Though I have met folks before who were afraid to tell their true name, so I am content to wait until you feel safe before hearing yours."

It is his turn to be startled. She obviously knows he has not used their true names, but is not concerned about it. With a touch, he wakes Clola and sets her on his lap. She protests for a moment and then looks into his eyes, after a glance at the woman before them.

"See, I told you there was no reason for hiding our names. It is really quite safe," Clola says, trying to settle back to sleep.

"Are you sure? This is not what Merry taught me," he says privately, shaking her to make her remain wakeful. "Stay awake, I need you now."

"Oh, alright," the dragon says crossly. "But I can hear just as well asleep as awake, you know." Turning her jewelled eyes to the waiting wise woman she says, "Thank you, Balgavney. My true name is Clola. He can tell you his own when he decides to quit being so stubborn." The little dragon settles with her eyes half-closed on the man's lap.

Balgavney smiles at the small dragon and says gravely, "Men are like that, you know. I greet you, Clola." The wise woman winks at Paddler, who is feeling a bit cross. He is hesitant to give his name, even with reassurance from Clola. The habit of protecting it has been life-long and he still hears Merry's voice telling him to never use it around strangers.

Taking a deep breath, he decides that life is about learning and sometimes a risk must be taken. "I am called Kemnay," he says, sounding a bit strangled.

Balgavney looks at him with her sparkling green eyes and says seriously, "I greet and welcome you, Kemnay."

The heavens do not open up, the ground does not shake; all remains as it was in the quiet place they are sitting. Kemnay releases his held breath in relief. Another lesson added to the many he already carries. Clola just nudges him on the arm and settles back to being half asleep.

Balgavney dips her face to hide for a moment behind her sleeve and suppresses a giggle. He is so serious, yet she heard his laughter through the trees earlier. An interesting mixture of impressions he gives. She hopes he will stay for a while, at least long enough to figure out a way to come over the hill.

She turns her body so that she is facing the statue at the bottom of the hill, takes another breath and tells him her story.

Balgavney's story

"This is my eighth incarnation as Balgavney, the wise woman of Wolf Angel Isle. I was an old woman of five and seventy storm seasons in my first incarnation in this place, when the disaster happened." Her voice is level and calm.

Once again Kemnay is taken by surprise. From Merry he knows that souls that have chosen to follow the wise path are always reborn as wise ones in a village. However, it is unusual for them to be the same person over and over, or even in the same place. Merry had told him that most folks lived on the path of rebirth, until they learned enough to choose their next form of incarnation or were forced by the gods to become dead-end souls, forever lost. Wise ones are sent to where their talents could give the most to help. For Balgavney to still be here is a bit worrying, especially for so long.

Balgavney's voice continues, ignoring his surprise for now. "When I was fifty storm seasons old, a lone woman in our village showed signs of being with child. The woman, Rora Moss, was a tailor of fantastic skill. She had lived alone all of her adult life. None of the men would say that it was his, nor did she ever tell who the father was, until it was too late. At the time there were many travellers that would visit, and the villagers assumed one of them had caught her fancy. As you know, no child is refused and parentage is not so much a concern, except for matters of celebration and congratulations.

"One particular traveller, who had come through the village earlier, was suspected of being the father. He was a tall, dark-skinned man with an uncertain temper, a trader of fabrics and threads, who often would visit Rora Moss. He could be gentle and friendly and in the blink of an eye angry and shouting, or sitting in a corner weeping. It was felt he had gotten too close to the gods and been touched by them. In many ways, he and Rora Moss were alike. He was just called Trader and would never admit to a true name.

"Rora Moss had wished for a family, but had never found a man who could deal with her total fear of the sea. At the time we were mostly fisher-folk and our village was a haven for traders and travellers. We have kith and kin on many of the local isles and often would travel by boat. It was not unusual for folks to marry across isles and move, or just visit frequently. However, Rora Moss could not even stand the sound of the sea and a walk near the pier made her faint. She even had a house built at the top of the village to be as far from the sea as she could, making sure no windows or doors opened to look over it."

Kemnay looks at her questioningly. She smiles and continues, "Yes, the house where the children found you was hers."

"One stormy night, I heard a scratching at my door, and when I opened it a great black wolf came in and sat by my fire. When it spoke to me, I knew it was a companion, so I welcomed it and fed it. Our village had a bonded pair for protection, but the man had found a mate on another isle and wanted to move away. The gods would not leave us unprotected so we requested they send another pair. This wolf was the answer to our request, or so I thought at the time.

"The wolf told me his name was Garmond. He told me he was sent to bond with the unborn girl-child Fintray. I welcomed his news with great joy. It would allow the man Pitsligo and his greyhound companion Duffus to go across the water and marry, while keeping our isle protected.

"When I asked Garmond the name of the child's mother, to my surprise he told me that it was Rora Moss. He explained she was to become a last-life soul, so he would not be able to speak to her after the child was born. He asked me to introduce Rora Moss to him and to help teach the child. Considering her fears, I was surprised she was to become a last-life soul. It is unusual for that change to happen during a person's lifetime. However, her joy in her talent was greater than her fear, so I felt the balance was in order. I accept that the gods know more than I am allowed to know." The wise woman pauses for a moment and goes on sadly, "I didn't ask enough questions of Garmond, until it was too late."

At this point Kemnay interrupts, "Last-life soul? I have never heard of such. I know of dead-end souls, who have been removed from the wheel as punishment by the gods."

It is Balgavney's turn to look surprised and just as confused as Kemnay feels. "Dead-end souls? I have never heard of such. Souls don't die. The gods do not force folks off the wheel. They will allow them to leave, for a while, if they are not strong enough for rebirth. However, these souls are expected to return and finish their learning when they are ready. They often will come back as the companion half of a bonded pair -- a much more powerful, yet more demanding incarnation, and often a longer incarnation than simple rebirth.

"When a soul has learned all it needs, or has reached a point where its suffering is less than its joy, it is given the choice to retire from the wheel into the quiet lands or to join the wise ones and help others. These are what I mean when I say when I say last-life soul," Balgavney says in a teaching voice.

The wise woman continues, "These people are usually very talented, happy and loved. Their life is a gift to their community and themselves. They give balance to those who still struggle and learn. They give the rest hope and knowledge of what learning there is to have in their lives and the reward that awaits them."

Kemnay is astonished. His voice is strained as he replies to her, "You are telling me that what I have known all my life, the dead-end souls for whom I have grieved, is actually a good thing?"

Balgavney frowns and gives him a quizzical look. She turns to the small dragon and asks, "Clola, what is he talking about?"

Clola nods to the wise woman, then looks up at her bonded companion and says, "Remember Merry told you that her own teaching had been broken and much of what she had learned was confused? Always be ready for a new idea, or to have an old idea reborn. Listen, open your mind and listen to this woman. She tells you the truth. There is a reason the gods led us here."

"But Clola," he protests, "You never told me any of this. You never argued with Merry."

The small dragon shrugs. "You never asked. We often argued, just never within your hearing. Merry does her very best for your village even with her broken knowledge. But this woman," the dragon inclines her head at Balgavney, "has had unbroken teaching from the gods. Learn from her so that you may return and help Merry, if you wish to." Clola yawns and settles back on his lap with her eyes half-lidded.

After this succession of revelations, he finds his throat is dry and his mind in a whirl. He takes the water skin off his belt and unties it, takes a big drink and absently offers it to Balgavney. Then his hand hits the magic barrier and he remembers that he can't share. Embarrassed by his confusion, he whispers, "I'm sorry."

The wise woman smiles sadly and lifts her own water skin for a drink. She worries about the level of shock this traveller is showing. If it were not for Clola, she would be surprised to find him bonded. He seems so very young. "I am sorry to have distressed you, Kemnay, though I fear it will not be the last time I do so as we talk," Balgavney says quietly.

New revelations

Kemnay suddenly gets up from the boulder, dropping Clola, who squawks in protest. He turns his back on Balgavney and starts to pace, but he can't decide where to go. Should he flee back to his boat or down to the village or stay? He is shocked by what the wise woman has said and afraid that the rest of her story will be even more unsettling for him. All his life's learning is being turned inside out and he isn't sure what to think. He knows he must hear the rest of it, because without her knowledge he will be unable to heal what is wrong here, but at this moment he is not sure he is ready to hear more.

Kemnay fights the urge to go down the hill, get back in his boat, leave this place and never look back. He knows he will not be able to do that. He is held here by magic and while it can't hurt him, at least physically, it will not allow him to leave without doing what he has promised. Besides, he honestly wants to help these people, and he can't do that if he leaves. Bowing his head, he again pleads with his gods for help, knowing that the help they are offering comes from the woman patiently waiting for him to decide what to do, and it is going to hurt even more before she is finished.

Clola, annoyed at being dropped so suddenly, comes over to him, shifts slightly larger and bites him quite hard on the tender place at the back of his knee. Lost in his thoughts, he is caught by surprise and cries out, pulling away from her and promptly trips over the boulder he had been sitting on, landing in a heap in the grass. He hears Balgavney's laughter and his face flushes again. This woman surely believes him to be a total klutz. He turns automatically holding up his arms in defence. Many times he has fought with Clola, and many times they both ended up bruised and slightly bloody. He doesn't want to fight with her right now; it won't help.

In the meantime, Clola is trying to take another bite out of him. He holds a hand up to her and says, "Enough. I know you are annoyed with me, but enough. Not now, Little One."

The dragon hesitates for a moment, glowering at him, then turns her back on him and spreads herself over the top of the boulder. Her actions tell him he had best choose to sit on the ground or risk a further tussle with the irritated dragon.

Balgavney, in the meantime, is laughing helplessly. "Why is it," he asks crossly, sitting on the ground out of reach of the boulder, "that all wise women find it so easy to laugh at me?" He remembers Merry and Achath frequently laughed at the problems he had while dealing with the dragon's uncertain temper.

Balgavney takes a moment to check her laughter and wipe her eyes. "I'm sorry, Kemnay," she says, "it is just that you are the first bonded pair I have met that argue so." Her cheeks are rosy from the laughter and the colour makes her brilliant eyes all the more beautiful. "I will say in truth," she admits, "most bonded pairs bring laughter to wise folk, in one way or another. Their personality mix is often comic to hide a deeper power."

"Take Pitsligo and Duffus. Pitsligo is a serious young man who is a teacher of children and a keeper of records. Duffus, as a greyhound, is silly-looking to start with, but he is also the most uncoordinated creature I have ever known. He trips over his own shadow, often hits his head on doors and if he falls into the water he has to be rescued, because he can't swim. As a magical creature, he can't drown, of course, but once he spent three hours in the bay waiting for someone who was willing to brave the cold water to help him out." Balgavney's voice is cheerful with memory.

Kemnay looks surprised. "You are teasing me to make me feel better," he says, as he shifts into the grass closer to the boulder where Clola is sleeping. He makes sure to nudge her so she knows he is there. In response, she pokes him with a claw until he moves so he is not casting his shadow over her.

Balgavney lifts an eyebrow. "Honestly, I am not at all," the wise woman says. "What you should also know is that these two maintain all the routes over the water on the other side of the hill, between the many isles, and provide safe passage even in the season of storms. Together they are very strong.

"They are a very powerful pair, though to look at them you would never know it. Neither of them is an obvious choice for life on the sea. Pitsligo is a small man with thin hair. He catches cold easily and can be very nervous, but he is the most skilled sailor in the village. Duffus not only can't swim, but is as near to stupid as can be, though he is a very loveable creature. His coat is an amazing mix of colours, as if the gods could not decide which would suit him best. Actually, it matches his personality -- beautiful, but disordered." The wise woman's voice had a hint of curiosity in it..

"They are part of the chain of pairs that have been our protection in these isles for a long time. Some say they have protected us since the gods tore the lands apart and made all the world into islands. Who knows?" The wise woman shrugs. "I have known them all my lives and they are just as stuck in this place as myself and the rest of the folks from this isle."

Lunch interlude

From over the hill come the sound of voices, breaking into the serious conversation they are having. Balgavney and Kemnay are grateful for the respite and turn to see Tifty, Ythsie and Skene approaching. Tifty is carrying another basket, Skene and Ythsie have a jug between them and cups in each outside hand. The three of them stop in front of Balgavney.

"I figured you would need a break from all the talking, as well as some food and drink," Tifty says, slightly breathless. She turns to the children, and orders, "Set that down, now and go after the other basket." The children set the jug and cups down carefully at Balgavney's feet, then scamper towards Paddler.

Clola, hearing their voices, raises up her head. Ythsie stops and rubs the dragon between her jewelled eyes. Clola bumps the child with her forehead, hoping for more pumpkin candy. Ythsie whispers, "I have some for you for later, but you should have lunch first. Mama says." Her small face is dirty and serious. Clola bumps her on the forehead again and the child giggles.

"Ok, Ythsie, I will wait," Clola says resignedly.

Meanwhile, Skene has picked up the basket sitting by Paddler and nearly fallen over. "It's empty, Mama," the boy says.

"Well of course it is, child. I expected that. It will be full of yesterday's dishes, which you'll be washing later," Tifty says matter-of-factly.

Paddler leans over to the child and whispers to him, "I washed all the dishes, Skene, not to worry." The child's face breaks into a sunny smile. Skene carefully takes the basket back to his mother, who spreads out a blanket on the grass and starts unpacking her basket.

Balgavney goes over to help, but Tifty waves her aside, telling her, "The best help you can be, woman, is to sit there out of the way now." The inn keeper points to a corner of the blanket. Tifty pauses for a moment and frowns, then says, "Well, I suppose you could pour some ale for Paddler, so that one of the children can carry it over."

Balgavney takes the jug, removes the stopper, lines up the cups and pours into each expertly. Soon a lovely head of foam is on the top of the three mugs. The children are each carrying a skin, which most likely have water in them.

After a few moments the foam recedes a bit, so Balgavney picks up a mug and carefully hands it to Skene. Ythsie has a plate with sandwiches, vegetables and fruits that she carries towards Paddler, walking carefully after her brother. Clola sits up on the boulder and watches the children closely, for she is of a mind to eat all the lunch, leaving Paddler hungry for tormenting her earlier.

Paddler reaches for the mug and the plate, thanking the children happily. Clola shifts larger and makes to attack the plate, but before she can move towards it Tifty says firmly, "Now wait a moment here, Little One, I understand you are fond of pumpkin."

Clola checks her motion suddenly and looks over at Tifty, who has taken a steaming baking dish out of the bottom of the basket. Now alert, the dragon tries to fly that direction and hits the magic barrier. Clola is stunned for a moment and lands in a heap on the ground. There are assorted giggles as the dragon picks herself up and shifts smaller again. Hopping from foot to foot, radiating impatience, she waits. Ythsie and Skene go over to their mother and take the dish, carefully wrapped in cloth, as well as a small jug of milk. They carry these over to where Clola is bouncing around. In the meantime Paddler takes advantage of her distraction and starts eating his meal rapidly.

Balgavney says quietly to him, "Slow down, you are going to choke." The wise woman is astonished at the obviously well-practised speed the man eats with.

Paddler shakes his head and takes a quick drink of the strong ale. "I have learned not to choke, and I learned when I was young to eat very fast, especially if I have annoyed her." He nods his head towards the dragon. "She won't let me starve, but she is not averse to making me go hungry." He returns to eating quickly.

Balgavney just laughs and shakes her head as she turns to her own meal. There is great joy in this pair, despite the friction between them.

The children carefully set the baking dish down, uncover it, and retreat quickly. Inside is a casserole of pumpkin, meat and spices. The dragon is beside herself with joy and immediately shoves her face into it. She has to pause for a moment because it is very hot, and though her body is well armoured with scales, the inside of her mouth can be a bit tender. She sticks her head into the milk jug and cools her tongue. After a few moments she returns to the casserole a bit more cautiously. After a few bites she looks up at Paddler and says, "Tifty is a much better cook than you are. I think I'll go and live with her."

Paddler says wryly, "I admit I don't have a proper oven and may not be the best cook, but I have never starved you. If you want to abandon me now, go ahead." It is empty threats on both sides, as they cannot be separated except by the gods, and that would result in their deaths.

"Thank you, Little One," Tifty says proudly. "That casserole is my own secret recipe. I am also fond of pumpkins." The inn keeper gives the children each a plate of food and is settling down with her own. They eat in comfortable silence, with low, contented growls coming from Clola.

Paddler finishes his meal and settles back with the mug of ale. This he can enjoy slowly because Clola hates even the smell of it. She won't even tip over his cup for fear of accidentally stepping in it. When he really wants to annoy her he will cook with it and make her hunt her own dinner. He can't shift size, but he is clever in his other ways and sometimes holds his own against the small dragon.

Clola has already finished the meal, licked the dish clean, and started to chew on the rim when Tifty says sharply, "Now see here, little dragon, don't you be breaking my best dish. I'll not cook for you again if you do."

Clola instantly lets go of it and nudges it up to the barrier. Ythsie comes after the dish and the empty milk jug and takes them back to her mother. Clola flops belly up in the sun and lets out an enormous burp. She has had pumpkin twice in one day and she is very happy. She has even forgiven Paddler for dumping her on the ground, though she won't actually say it so he can hear.

Skene giggles at the flopped dragon. She looks at him with one jewelled eye and sticks out her tongue. Balgavney grins as she turns to Tifty and ask the inn keeper, "Have you ever in your life seen such a silly creature? Clola reminds me of Duffus, except she seems a bit more co-ordinated."

"Every bonded pair I've met, in all my times, has always been keen for good food and plenty of it. I expect changing size and shape or making strong magic makes food more important," Tifty says wisely. "Though I agree with you that I don't at all understand why Duffus is such a klutz. Their magic is strong indeed."

Clola doesn't move from her sunny place, but says, "Duffus is in the wrong form. He was suppose to be a grey hawk, not a hound, but he made the air gods angry before his form was set, so they grounded him."

"That would explain quite a lot," Balgavney says, thoughtfully smiling.

Tifty snorts with laughter and says, "My children, I expect it is time for us to get back to work. Enough of this lagging about in the sun." She starts to gather dishes and linens up into the basket.

In chorus the two children protest, "But Mama, what about dessert?"

Tifty rolls her eyes. "Did I not feed you enough lunch? Now you want a dessert as well?" Even as their mother is speaking, she is bringing more things out of her seemingly bottomless basket.

The woman hands a sweet pastry to Skene and some candies to Ythsie. "Now share those with our guests, and then you can have yours," she orders.

The children walk over to Paddler, and give him the pastry. Clola rolls over and receives the candied pumpkin. There are three pieces of it, so she takes one in each claw and has Ythsie put one in her mouth. She bumps the child with her forehead and says to Tifty, "Thank you, good woman. You are the greatest of cooks."

Paddler is busy enjoying the pastry which is filled with apples and berries. He nods his thanks while stuffing his mouth. The children each receive a small pastry, while Balgavney has some of the candied pumpkin. Tifty looks well-pleased and gathers up all the rest of the dishes and linens.

Skene returns to Paddler to get the plate and mug, which he hastily empties. The man is not in a hurry to return to talking with Balgavney and is grateful for the respite of other people's company, as well as the good meal.

Tifty looks up at him for a moment and says knowingly, "I expect this conversation is not easy for either of you. The telling of it is hard and I expect the hearing of it is much harder." Both Paddler and Balgavney nod.

"Somewhat like your choices of husbands, Tifty?" Balgavney teases gently

Tifty coughs and says, "Well, this one has been better than the others."

Balgavney cannot resist, "Indeed? Rather like deciding if spiders are better than slugs for supper."

As Tifty begins to protest, Clola says loudly, "Slugs, of course. There is more meat to them. Spiders are too small, though they are nice and crunchy...." She burps again.

Ythsie says, "Eww!" very loudly and makes gagging noises.

Tifty says wryly, "Little One, I don't think I needed to know that. Now, it is time to be gone, children. We will bring up supper for you three later."

Paddler protests, "Tifty, you are too kind. We cannot as now repay all that you have done for us. We are deeply in your debt."

Tifty looks at him sternly. "Youngling, I am on my eighth incarnation as the inn keeper. While it is a nice enough job, I would very much like to change for my next incarnation. If you will be good enough to solve this problem over here, so that I can go on, to a new rebirth, you will earn more meals than I can ever feed you, or your bottomless wee lass there." The woman points to Clola, who burps again.

The inn keeper gathers the baskets, gives each of the children various jugs or mugs to carry and sets off over the hill.

Kemnay waits until the family is out of hearing, then looks at Balgavney in shock. "Her too?"

Balgavney looks at him sadly and says, "All of us. We are trapped here, any of us who are directly related to last-life souls, those who have been turned to stone. Until we can free them, we can never go on. Since this happened, we have not had another last-life soul in our village, nor can they cross the barrier. We are stuck in a cycle that we cannot break. You are the first new person to arrive on this side of the hill, in this bay, for nearly 800 seasons of storm. We dearly hope you can find the way to free us."

Kemnay is glad he is sitting, for this news makes him feel light headed and slightly sick. Though his own life is one that might be considered immortal, he knows that most folks on the wheel must go on to a new rebirth, to learn enough to reach the end. To be trapped in the same life, over and over, would be a kind of hell that makes his life look as easy as a baby's smile.

"I did not realise, Balgavney," he says seriously "I must know all that has happened so that I can do whatever I can to heal it. I'm sorry to know you are all trapped, and I will do my best to free you."

Clola climbs up on his lap and adds her voice to his. "The gods have sent us here, to you, for good reason. Do not worry, wise one, your faith is not wasted. Together we are blessed and can help." The dragon settles in Paddler's lap and waits for Balgavney to continue.

Balgavney resettles to the top of the sun-warmed boulder and asks him, "Are you sure you are ready for more? I feel as if I need to instruct you as I would any young bonded pair. Your knowledge seems confused."

Kemnay nods and shrugs. "Yes, my knowledge is confused, but I knew this from the onset. I must hear your story and though I fear it, I am ready. Don't worry, I am not quite as young as I seem." His manner is calm and reassuring.

Balgavney accepts what he says and carries on. "I was surprised to find Rora Moss was to become a last-life soul, and from what Garmond was telling me, it would occur during her life. This is very unusual. I knew he had contact with the gods and would know better than I, so I accepted what he told me without hesitation. Perhaps that was foolish of me, without having asked him more questions." The sadness on her face is painful to Kemnay and he closes his eyes for a moment to shield himself from her pain, then opens them again and smiles encouragingly at the beautiful woman.

Clola speaks to the wise woman softly. "You could not have known that Garmond was a rogue who slipped between the gods' fingers. Do not carry the burden that is not your own."

"Thank you, Clola," Balgavney says. "I have learned much since then, and been moved to despair and anger many times. Now I wish only to find forgiveness and to release all of us from our suffering."

"So your incarnations have not been wasted. I expect your next one will be gentler for you," Clola predicts.

"I can only hope and pray that it is so," Balgavney says honestly.

Kemnay waits, near to bursting with questions for both of them. He realises that he will have to let Balgavney move in the comfort of her own time, but tonight Clola is going to be seriously questioned. "Not to worry," the dragon says silently. "You will be ready for the answers by then."

The wise woman takes a deep breath and tells the rest of the story.

Rora Moss and Garmond

The next morning I took the wolf Garmond up to Rora Moss' house on the hill. She was sitting in the shadow of her house sewing, well out of sight of the sea. When I came around to her she looked startled for a moment, but then something in her totally relaxed. She said to Garmond, "You came. I wasn't sure, but here you are." She got up from her chair and hugged him tightly.

Garmond responded to her saying, "I promised you I would come and I will reward you as we bargained." At this, I began to be alarmed. Most women resist a companion and the knowledge it brings that their child is to be bonded, but Rora Moss seemed to be expecting this.

Garmond looked at me and said, "All is as it should be. You will be needed when the child is to be born, and to help teach her, but for now you can be gone." He shoved me out of the gate and made it clear I would not be permitted to return until he was ready to allow it.

I was a woman of middle years and used to accepting what the gods demanded of me. As strange as this was to me, I still did not suspect how truly terrible it would be.

I returned to my home and told Pitsligo that we had a new pair soon to be taught. He was delighted, but Duffus was strangely silent about it. I believe he knew something, but without the right questions could not tell me what I should have known. I have since learned to ask more questions.

Thus things went on as normal, then a few months later after the beginning of the season of the storms, Garmond was at my door, telling me it was time for the child and to come right away. It was a terrible night. I could not keep a torch lit in the rain and had to hang on to Garmond and have him all but drag me up the hill to where Rora Moss was labouring. He would not allow me to bring anyone else from the village to help, so alone I went up the hill in the storming darkness.

Rora Moss was laid out on the floor in front of the fire, obviously in great pain. I went to lift her off the floor and move her, but Garmond would not allow me to do this. Instead, I brought pillows and blankets to her and calmed her as much as I could. I made tea and set water to warming, made sure all that I needed for the child was at hand. Then I sat on the floor and spoke softly to her, while Garmond watched me closely, his wolf eyes glittering dangerously in the firelight. I was starting to be afraid and wondered if this would be the last night of my life.

Garmond looked at me, as if reading my mind, and said, "You are needed here and I cannot kill you, but it is well that you understand I would wish to, if the gods would allow me this. You and all of the others here, except this girl-child. At her wish, for her sake alone, life remains," he laughed deeply and wickedly.

I was not convinced he would actually harm anyone, but wasn't willing to take the chance. My oath requires me to help, where help is needed. I could deal with his threats later.

Then Rora Moss gasped in pain, reached out, and grasped hold of the wolf's head. "I am keeping my promise, you must keep yours," she cried.

"Yes, Rora Moss," the wolf said. "I have promised you that you will give your soul to this child and become a last-life soul. You will have a husband who loves you and many other good children. You will be happy and free of your fears." He glanced at me, nodding. "I need this child to survive, so that I may stay where the gods cannot reach me. With her bonded to me, they cannot send me into the darkness alone."

It is just as Clola has said -- he was a rogue. Sent into exile by the gods, sentenced not to be killed, but chained to the wheel with no prospect of leaving the chain of rebirth. To be caught in eternity without hope. He had made a terrible bargain, but I don't believe he was entirely bad. I think he was just afraid of being lost in the darkness.

There was nothing I could do but help Rora Moss give birth. There was no way to stop the frightening bargain she had made, for in truth it was not terrible. It was an act of desperation. She wanted a family and children, the joy that most folks take for granted, and to be freed from her fears. Even now I cannot say this is a dreadful thing.

For hours I sat with the labouring woman, holding her hand and offering comfort to her as I would to any woman in labour. Just before dawn the storms outside quieted and the wind stopped howling. Suddenly, it felt as if the world was holding its breath.

Garmond looked into Rora Moss' eyes and told her, "Now, it is time for this child. Bring her to me."

Rora Moss gave a great push and her daughter slid into my hands. I felt her soul transfer to the child, the exchange from the last-life soul in the child and felt the lock of bonding set at the same moment. Fintray was a beautiful dark-skinned child, with dark hair and storm grey eyes. Garmond bit through the cord and cleaned the child with his tongue. I set the child on a blanket near the fire and took care of resettling Rora Moss into her bed. She was suddenly alight with joy, such as I had never seen in her.

After the new mother was settled I took up the child and looked at her closely. She watched me with her serious newborn eyes and I felt the power in her. I set her to her mother's breast and returned to the hearth to speak more with Garmond.

"Garmond," I said, "tell me of this child and your bargain with Rora Moss. For now that is it started, I will need to know all I can to teach her."

Garmond settled in front of the fire and spoke softly and seriously to me. "As you suspected, I am a rogue spirit, born of one of the gods who touched a mortal. I was the one you called Trader, with the uncertain moods. My life was difficult as my mother would not speak of my father and the gods would not own up to me either. I could talk to all, but sometimes the noise in my head drove me near to madness. I had asked a wise woman far away what I could do. She told me that my only hope was to find a mortal woman and breed a child, bond with that child and have a respite and rest from the cycle of rebirth. She also told me that I would have to give much in return for this. So I stole a wish stone from the gods and fled into the world. This theft is what has condemned me, but my life was already hell, so I didn't fear more. After keeping the stone with me for some time, I realised it could restore my sanity, but without the child to hold me to the world, it wouldn't matter. I would still be cast into the darkness alone.

"So I wandered the world as Trader, until I came upon this place and met the woman Rora Moss. Her fears touched me deeply and her desires seemed so reasonable. I offered her a bargain: if she would bear me a child and let me bond with it, I would remove her fears and grant her a last-life soul, so she could have a happy family and finally retire to the quiet lands in peace. It seemed we were both to get a good bargain and no one was to be harmed.

"After the child was conceived, I went into hiding nearby, so that I could watch and be ready. At the time I knew to be right, I took the wish stone and told it all that I wanted. I invoked it and suffered the great pain of being changed into this form. I am allowed no other on my own. Once the stone had been invoked the gods knew what I had done, but they could not stop it if the child was born before dawn of the second day of the season of storms. As you see, I have won and now all will be well. I promise you that this child and I will protect this place well."

I nodded that I understood. I had heard of such bargains and had no doubt that the gods would honour it, but I also knew that the price for it would be great. This I feared, even if Garmond didn't seem to.

"Very well, Garmond," I said. "I will accept that you mean no harm and I will teach this child. What can you tell me of her?"

Garmond let his thoughts drift. "I am not totally certain, Balgavney. I know she will be able to change form, but only to one other. I don't know yet what that form will be, but it will be part of the protection we provide. I know she will have two great fears that she will deal with through her power, but the future is a blur to me. When I gave up my human form, I gave up all direct contact with the gods. I must now live within their rules as a companion in a bonded pair. I will have many answers, when they are needed, but not before."

I was tired and troubled. "Garmond, I must send another woman up to help care for Rora Moss and Fintray. I need rest in my own bed."

"Now that the child is safe born, the whole village can come. Set a day for naming," the wolf said as he went into the room to curl up with the girl-child and her mother to keep them warm.

As I stepped out the door, I realised the storm had stopped and the sun was shining. Very odd, but I was so tired it hardly mattered. I wandered down the hill, stopping at the stone circle to whisper the child's name to the gods, then went to the inn and found my daughter Skirza. I asked her to go up and watch over Rora Moss and the child until I had gotten some rest. She agreed and I returned to my home.

Young Fintray

The day was unusually clear, not that I noticed, sleeping through it as I did. That evening I went back up to find Rora Moss moving about her kitchen, looking rested and well -- not at all like a woman who had just given birth. She made me a cup of tea and we settled by the cradle to talk. The babe was restless when Rora Moss was more than a short distance from her.

"Isn't she beautiful, Balgavney?" Rora Moss asked me, her eyes shining.

"Yes, Rora Moss, she is indeed beautiful," I agreed. Whatever magic was here, I felt it was good and I relaxed into it. As I sat, I heard the wind start to rise outside and the child again became fretful.

Rora Moss took a cotton hat and covered the child's head and ears so that the sound was stopped for her. "Hush, little Fintray, this will make that bad sound go from your ears. Rest now, child," Rora Moss said. The babe immediately quieted. Turning to me Rora Moss said "She doesn't like the sound of the wind. Poor wee lass, born at the start of the season of storms. Well, all new babies have things that worry them, don't they?"

"I expect you are right, Rora Moss. Just keep her head covered and sing softly to her. I expect Garmond can sing to her as well." Garmond nodded from his place under the cradle and begin a deep rumbling song in his chest which filled the room comfortably.

A week or so later, there was a break in the weather and the entire village gathered at the stone circle to celebrate and name the new child. Her name, Fintray, was called out to the gods and all of us, while Rora Moss held her proudly and Garmond stood beside. There was much rejoicing and we all gathered at the inn for a good supper. Also there that night was a young man named Strathy, recently across from the outer isles. He was a tall, blond fellow of pleasing temper, and a very talented grower of vegetables. He was wandering from his home in hopes of finding a wife.

When the celebration reached the inn, suddenly he was in the middle of a village full of very happy folks. He looked over at Rora Moss and something in his eyes caught fire. Walking over to me he asked if he might be introduced to her. In the nature of happy celebration, I took him over to her.

"Rora Moss," I said gaily, "this is the traveller Strathy come to greet you and wish you well."

The young man held his hand out to her and for a moment they touched. He looked into her eyes as if he had found what he had wanted all his life. "I greet you, Rora Moss and your angel Fintray. I wish you a lifetime of happiness." With that he held out his hands and she slipped the babe into the cradle of his arms. He was the first person, other than myself, who had been allowed to hold the babe. If any other tried to touch her she became alarmed and fretful, but with this man she just looked into his eyes with love.

Her love was returned one hundred fold. This man loved her and her mother from the moment they met. The two of them married at the end of the season of the storms and within a year there was another baby in the house: a daughter, Tifty, who was a talented cook. In another year, a son, Helman. Their home was always full of laughter and joy.

I started teaching Fintray as soon as she could sit. She was fine with me as long as one or the other of her parents were close at hand, within her hearing, and it was not stormy outside. She was very fearful of storms. She also seemed unusually attached to her mother.

The only time she would go from her parents' sight was when she and Garmond would wander the fields. Even then, Fintray kept her home in sight, as if to lose it would be the end of her.

I spent many long days and seasons teaching her and she learned everything quickly.

When she was five storm seasons old, we walked down to the magic circle with Garmond, talking about speaking to the gods. She told me she didn't want the gods to notice her, which drew a nod from the wolf. I reassured her that they would not harm her.

I had seen no signs of shifting in her, but this day something felt different. While I stood watching her, she stood on top of a square stone and suddenly she had great feathered wings. "Look," the child said, "I'm an angel, just as papa always says I am."

"I can see that you are," I said, as calmly as I could. I turned to Garmond and asked, "Is this what you meant?"

"Yes, it is," the wolf said calmly, "but there is more."

He then walked up to her and seemed to melt into her. For an instant the two forms overlapped, then suddenly before me was the form of the Wolf Angel. They only held the pose for a few moments, but I realised that form was very strong. A melded bonded pair were the strongest known. Given enough time, they might even challenge the gods, but I could not say that to either of them. Fintray would not know to ask and Garmond could not remember until he was asked.

So, for a time, all was well in the village. Every season of storms seemed to be a little milder, at least for us. I didn't realise then that Fintray was learning to keep the storms away. As much as I could teach her, she learned a great deal on her own or from Garmond. The people of the village were adjusting to her wings, when she shifted to them, though as yet she had not taken flight.

When she had celebrated her tenth season of storms, she did something so remarkable that I think even Garmond was surprised. She asked the stone mason for a square stone set at the bottom of the fields to watch over the village. He was glad to oblige her, and soon her stone was set. She and Garmond called the village together and she shifted to her wings. Together with him, she stood on the top of the stone and they melded into their Wolf Angel form. Suddenly, the sky cleared back to the sea cliffs and to the top of the hill, as far as could be seen from the stone.

Her childish voice could be heard by all as she promised, "I will keep the storms away, so we can have another season of grain instead." Then she and Garmond stepped down, leaving the image of the statue that you have seen there now. I was astonished and walked up to her.

"Fintray, child, to have the grain we must have the rain from the sky," I told her kindly. "And sometimes the fields must rest a season."

"I can let rain come without the storm, just tell me when it is needed," she said in youthful arrogance. "The farmers are smart and know which fields to rest."

I could not fight her, and I could not change what she had done. We accepted it as a gift and the farmers made another crop. Whenever rain was needed, they would either ask Fintray directly or just go to the statue and say it out loud. Always just the rain would come, as much as was needed, but never did the wind howl. There was never more than a comfortable breeze. Later, the stone mason made small images of the statue so that each home could have one. Fintray touched each one and could hear any request made near them.

After five such seasons, we had become rich with grain and had many traders coming to visit. The village was thriving and it was felt that Fintray had been a great gift from the gods indeed. Pitsligo and Duffus moved to their love's isle and the lanes between the isles thronged with traffic.

As word of riches gets around, sometimes it falls to ears best left in silence. Raiders heard of our good fortune and tried to come into the bay. Fintray seemed to expect this and made her barrier stronger. She could read intentions and most souls. Few got past her barriers and those were easily chased off by our village guards. Raiders gave up after losing many ships on the rocks at the entry to the bay.

Life was well and our village prospered. With the easing of the storm seasons, even I felt more well, for as you know, storm can be hard on old bones and souls. I continued to teach Fintray what I could, but mostly I provided her with companionship.

As she grew older, she showed no signs that she wanted to be away from her parents, even though Tifty married the inn keeper's son, and was known far and wide as the best cook on the isle. Helman married a lass on another isle and brought her back with him. He is now a boot maker of great skill. Rora Moss and Strathy had several more children, all happy and talented. All was well until the last was born, and then things went wrong very quickly.

Fintray learns the truth

On that morning, I sat with Rora Moss while she laboured with her last child. It was in the middle of the season of storms. Rora Moss always had an easy time with her babies. I was just there to catch the wee one and spread the good news. Fintray seemed more distracted than usual and kept returning to her mother's side. She was obviously frightened, but I didn't know why.

After sending Fintray out to keep the other children busy for the fifth time, I walked out and asked her, "Fintray, child, what is bothering you so? You know your mama has no trouble with babies and is never short of love for any of you. Why are you so restless?"

"Balgavney, I am afraid because this child has a voice I can't hear. Lately I have found several that I can't hear, including my mother and father, and it concerns me. I only just realised I can hear you, no matter where you are, but some people I can only hear if they speak." Fintray was distressed

"Do not be afraid child, I can explain this. Tomorrow I will tell you, but I promise you it is not a terrible thing," I said to her reassuringly.

"Alright, Balgavney, I will wait," she said, resigned, and smiled wistfully. "This is the first time I have not known the babe's name before mama."

I realised as I returned to Rora Moss that I had never explained about last-life souls to Fintray. She had never seemed to notice or had never asked before. I suspected some mischief from the gods, but was busy with the new baby. I should have been more cautious.

That afternoon, the girl-child Cullerlie was born. She was a beautiful and happy child, whom I knew would be the last for them, though I didn't realise why, to my later sorrow. Their joy in her was great, as it was in all their children. Fintray was just as delighted with her new sister as her parents. I felt that the family had been well-blessed by the gods.

The next morning, I met Fintray in the meadow near the magic circle and asked her how she had come to notice the voices she couldn't hear.

She told me she and Garmond had been walking along the shore when a great sea creature put up its head and asked if she was the "All Powerful Fintray, Coward of the Isles."

Fintray was annoyed at being mocked so. "I am Fintray and this is Garmond, and who are you that speaks so unkindly to me? I have done you no harm, why do you mock me?"

"I am sent by the water goddess as a friend to the wind gods, whom you offend by presuming to keep them away. I am to warn you that your companion is a villain and he will steal all that you love," the creature said with cruelty. Fintray looked at the creature, shocked and gave Garmond a puzzled look.

Garmond said to her, "Fintray, this is one who seeks to hurt you by making me seem untrustworthy. I have never in all of our time together led you to danger or hurt. Close your ears and let us leave this place. It is only mischief from those who are not so strong as you." Garmond was afraid, but his voice didn't show it.

Fintray knelt and hugged Garmond and turned back to the sea. "I do not believe you, foul monster," she cried out to the sea creature. "Garmond is my friend, my protector, and you are just an evil beast that needs be gone from here." She reached to reinforce her barrier to push out this creature from the bay.

Feeling the unstoppable push of her powerful magic, the beast spoke quickly, "Stay your hand a moment, child. You think I lie to you. Go into your village and find all the voices you cannot hear, the ones to whom you are deaf as an old woman. The ones you most fear to lose, this creature will steal."

Fintray was beside herself with anger and fear. She strengthened her ward to push the mocking creature away. The creature could only fight for another moment and it cried out, "They can't hear you either. You are nothing to them." Then it was gone beyond the barrier of the cliffs.

With Garmond following her, she ran, fast as summer lightning, back to the village. There, she realised that there were many souls she could not speak to. Among them was my daughter Skirza, who had been a friend to her all her life, and many others. Worst of all, her parents were in this deaf place, as well as the new child that was to be born. She was terrified by the realisation that many that she loved couldn't hear her. What she didn't try was to speak to them, so that she did not know that the sea beast had only told her half-truths.

She begged Garmond to explain, but the gods had made him unable to remember. He told her that she must ask me, that I would know. Deep within himself, he was afraid that he had hurt Fintray in some way he could not mend.

After hearing her story, I took her in my arms and held her like a small child, even though she was a woman of five and twenty storm seasons. "Child, child, don't be afraid," I crooned to her. "It is alright, that was a spirit of mischief sent to frighten you. It is not so bad a thing as the monster has said."

After long minutes of helpless sobbing, held between Garmond and I, Fintray finally started to come into control of her feelings, but her fear was still great. "Why can't they hear me, Balgavney?" she begged me. "How can those I love best be deaf to me?"

Looking at her distraught face, I wanted to go find that lying beast and do it hurt, despite my wisdom and oaths. This was more than simply mischief . I was sure the bargain made between Rora Moss and Garmond was the root of it, but I could not curse them, or even find them in error. Good had come of both of them and both had provided so much benefit to the village.

From my pocket I took a small bottle of mixture that I keep for such moments. I pulled out the dropper and ordered Fintray, "Child, open your mouth and take this. It will calm you so that you can hear me over the noise of your fright." A long habit of obedience made her do as I wished and I was able to give her some of the potion. After a short time, she was much calmer and, I felt, more able to hear me.

What I didn't realise, at that time, was just how deep her fears were and why. Had I known, I think I would have been more careful in my explanations to her. I have not learned to guard truth, often to my sadness. I tell what I know and expect to be heard, and too often this makes people around me very unhappy.

"Fintray," I said, "you must understand souls are different in each person. Most souls require rebirth so that they can learn the lessons that they need. Sometimes it takes many times on the wheel for one small lesson and there are many to learn. I, as a wise woman, have chosen to be chained to the wheel for all time, to teach and to guide, until all others are free from suffering that requires rebirth. Souls like yours and Garmond's are bonded, linked together to make something stronger. This is a serious responsibility chosen by both of you and it will be long, perhaps infinitely long, until either of you are given back to rebirth."

Fintray was calm, but within her there was a core of alarm, realising that she would live for a very long time.

I continued, very matter-of-factly. "There are also souls that have worked through all their lessons and become free of suffering. These souls are called last-life souls and they have this last rebirth to life to celebrate and demonstrate to the rest the ultimate reward of learning and rebirth. These souls are freed from being chained to the wheel or to each other. They live happy lives, that give hope to others. When their life is done they can choose to follow the wise path, as I have done, and help others to reach this place, or they are allowed off the wheel into the quiet lands. These souls are not heard by bonded ones, or wise ones, and some say that even the gods are deaf to them, because they have gone beyond all of us and have no need of our counsel. They can hear you, of course, dearest Fintray they can hear you. They know your love, but their lives are done, their souls are finished."

Horror welled up in her eyes. "You mean, Balgavney," she said in a choked voice, "that I will live beyond all those I love? I will be abandoned and left behind? That my mother, father, sister and friends will never be back?"

"Fintray," I said as gently as I could, "child, realise that this is the natural order of life. We are all of us, at one time or another, left behind. In our own time we will leave others behind as well. It is the way the wheel works for all living things. These souls have earned their rest."

I touched her hand. "Look at me. I am very old, and someday soon this life will be done for me. I will return reborn in another place, as another person, but still the wise woman, with other people to help."

"Balgavney, you can't leave me," she pleaded. "Say this is all just a story. What will I do without my mother or my father or my friends? I will perish!" She was becoming more and more agitated.

Trying my best to calm her, I said soothingly, "Child, hush, child. All of us lose our mothers, as our children lose us in our time. This is not the end. There will come a time when you join your parents again."

Once again Fintray was sobbing, "I can't lose my mother, I can't. You don't understand, I have to make her stay. There has to be some way to make her stay with me." Her eyes were hysterical.

I took her firmly by the shoulders and shook her, trying to break through her mounting hysteria. I did not understand why she was so distraught. I glanced at Garmond and he was looking at her and I with great guilt in his eyes. In silent talk, I demanded he help me get her to rest and then come speak with me about this. He nodded to me and went to her.

"Wingling," he said calmly, "this is not a worry for today. Today we are celebrating the birth of your new sister. There are many long years to worry about being left. Calm yourself, wipe your eyes, for your mother will be unhappy if she sees tears upon your face."

Between Garmond and myself we managed to get Fintray back up to Rora Moss. At the house, her mother settled the new baby into Fintray's arms and then sent us off. Rora Moss had a feeling something was wrong, and we needed to talk, but for the moment was just content watching her daughters.

Garmond and I returned to my house and I gave him a meal. After we had finished I asked him, "Garmond, what have you not told me that I am needing to know now? Why is Fintray so upset by the last-life souls? She acts like she has never heard of them, and I thought I had explained to her. It is such basic information."

Garmond settled before my fire with his great head upon his paws. "Actually, you haven't. It has never come up and you were left to assume she knew. It was hidden from her for good reason, but hidden things have a way of coming back to hurt us. Balgavney, you know the trade that was made when Fintray was born."

I nodded, looking at him with serious eyes. I would never forget that night. He continued, "Well, the gods allowed the trade of the last-life soul for the soul that could be bonded only because I forced it with the wish stone. Part of the price was to take Rora Moss' original fear and to add a second to it. This was passed to the child, so Fintray is afraid of the wind, but she is also afraid of losing her mother, as afraid of it as ever Rora Moss was of the sea."

I was aghast. Rora Moss had not been only afraid of the sea, but deadly terrified of it. For Fintray to be as afraid of losing her mother, when her mother had become a last-life soul, was a serious problem indeed. It was absolute that Rora Moss would die in her time and retire to the quiet lands. She had no interest in the wise way, she only wanted peace away from life. Fintray was going to lose her, not only in this life, but for all time and there was nothing I could do to change it. From the sorrow in Garmond's eyes, I realised he had been given no control of the outcome of the bargain. He had done the best he could and protected himself from exile, but the cost the gods had demanded for this was enormous and wicked.

"Garmond," I asked him, "what can we do? How can we ease this fear in her?" I was seriously hoping that there was a way to save this situation, which felt more and more dreadful with each passing moment.

He looked at me sadly. "There is nothing I can do. Any knowledge I had from my human form is hidden from me. I expect there is or will be a bonded pair that will be able to help, but I am unsure. I don't think it will be soon or even before Fintray's fear overwhelms her. Balgavney, I am afraid for Fintray. She is so powerful and her fear makes her power even stronger, but I can't guide or control this fear of hers. I quiet it as much as I can, distract her when I can, but it will not be enough. In the end I fear for her sanity. To block out the winds was easy, but her fear for her mother's loss, this is beyond me. I just do not know what to do."

"All we can hope for is that her mother will live a long time while we try to figure this out," I said, but in my heart I had a deep feeling of dread.

"No matter how long it is, it will not be long enough. You can not solve this, Balgavney, it is not your task, though you may have a hand in it," Garmond said. "I must return to Fintray now. She is very near the edge of her ability to cope. I must safeguard her and all of you."

I gave him a hug, let him out of the door and walked over to the home where my daughter Skirza lived. She was a last-life soul and I wanted to talk to her. She had not yet decided if she would remain on the wheel as a wise woman or retire to the quiet lands. I remembered my own time of choosing and rejoiced in being able to help her with hers.

Skirza walked back with me to my home. We sat together quietly talking, drinking tea and sharing laughter. It was the last evening I spent with my daughter and the memory of it still brings me to tears.

While we talked, Garmond returned to Fintray. She held the babe up for him to nuzzle and he pronounced her little, but was willing to curl around her and sing. Rora Moss was resting by the hearth while Strathy made a meal in the kitchen. The house was merry with laughter and joy at the new child.

Rora Moss was looking happily at her new child and her oldest one as well. She remembered the night Fintray was born and the wonderful feeling of being freed of her terrible fear of the sea. She knew that Fintray was afraid of the wind, but she did not realise that there was a second, even stronger fear. Nor did she know that the fears where linked or why. She just assumed all folks were afraid of something, and some fears were just stronger than others.

Rora Moss smiled at Fintray, just as Fintray looked over at her. "What is making you smile, mother?" Fintray asked, curious about the look in her mother's eyes. She was still worried about what Balgavney had said, but was willing to wait to learn more. There had to be a way to save her mother and her friends, she was sure of it. This thin thread of hope was all that she had.

"Fintray, child, I was just remembering the night you were born. There was a such great storm and then suddenly it was quiet, and there you were with your beautiful eyes," Rora Moss said. She smiled at Garmond, who was laying quietly with Cullerlie by the fire. "That night my life changed. I used to be afraid of the sea, now that fear is only a memory to me. How grateful I am to Garmond for taking that from me and giving you to me." Her loving eyes looked at the companion on the floor with gratitude.

Fintray looked puzzled "You were afraid of the sea?" she asked with surprise. "But you love the sea, you walk by it every day." The young woman had never known her mother to be troubled by anything.

Garmond's ears perked up as he looked from the young woman to the older one, and his body started to tense. Cullerlie became fretful at his change in mood and began to cry. Strathy came over and lifted her to his chest, and sat on the hearth holding her to him and rocking her gently to sleep. He listened closely to his wife's quiet voice. He could see Fintray was upset, but didn't understand why.

"Indeed I was afraid of it. Have you never noticed that this house is as far from the sea as you can be, still within the valley? That there are no windows or doors on that side of the house? Have you never been curious about it?" Rora Moss asked.

Fintray shook her head in negation and shrugged. "This has always been my home. I guess I never really thought about it being far away or different." She looked around the familiar room and smiled softly. "It is just home."

Rora Moss told Fintray, "Oh, child, I was so frightened by even the sound of the sea I could not stand to be near it. To walk along the pier would make my head spin and I would often faint. I never went near it if I could avoid it." Laughing softly, she continued, "I had made bargains with everyone in town so as to avoid going anywhere near the sea. Fortunately, Skirza would often run errands for me."

Fintray asked, "How did you overcome your fear, mother? This would be good for me to learn." Her distress was beginning to build as she thought of her own fears.

Rora Moss was lost in her memory and still didn't realise her daughter's fears. "In a way, you cured me of it, my darling child," she said in a far away voice.

Fintray's brow creased in perplexity. "What did I do?" she asked. She had done much magic to help the people of the village, but she did not remember doing this for her mother. She looked at Garmond, who would not meet her eyes.

"With Garmond's help, we traded souls. You were a last-life soul and we were allowed a trade so that you could be bonded with Garmond. When we traded souls, my fears went away and my life became wonderful and all that I could have ever hoped or dreamed of," Rora Moss said in a cheerful voice. "I gained a beautiful, talented child, then after you were born, a husband, and then a family. All that I had ever dreamed of and wished for." She smiled at Strathy, who lovingly returned her gaze, while absently kissing his new baby on the forehead.

"What?" Fintray shouted in alarm "We traded souls? How can that be? Balgavney never told me of this." She made as if to leave her chair.

Garmond stood up and put his paws on her to make her remain sitting. "Balgavney did not know the whole of it. Do not blame her. If there is blame, it is mine." He looked into her eyes, willing her to stay calm and try to understand. "Do not be afraid, I promise we will work it out." Secretly, he was not so sure, as the gods did not love him and the price of his theft was beginning to look very dear indeed.

Fintray in a panic

Reeling from what her mother was saying, Fintray asked, "But if the husband came later," she pointed at Strathy, "who is my father?" He had been the only father she had ever known and the idea that he was not hers was another shock to an already frightening day. She felt as if her heart would explode with confusion and terror.

Strathy said softly, looking at her with the love that was always in his eyes for her. "You are the child of my heart always, Fintray. I have loved you from the first moment I set eyes on you. It matters not who your father was, child." His acceptance and depth of love touched her even through her fears. This man loved her beyond anything and that was a gift in her life.

Rora Moss finally noticed the strength of Fintray's distress. "Now Fintray, child, you need to calm yourself. This is not so--" she started, but Fintray interrupted. She managed to get up from the chair, but Garmond tripped her and held her on the floor.

"Who is my father? Why did I have no say in the trading of souls? What is going on?" She was struggling against Garmond, but he would not let her come to her feet. He could not hurt her, but he could hold her in place as long as she was distracted.

Rora Moss knelt beside the two of them struggling on the floor and reached a hand to wipe the tears off of Fintray's face. Her face sad and worried for her daughter's reactions, which she didn't understand. The look of sorrow in her eyes made the young woman stop her shouting and try to reassure her mother. "I'm sorry, mother. Of course you can have my soul, if it makes you happy, you can have anything. Even Garmond." She was contrite.

Her mother smiled gently and patted Garmond on the head. "No, my dearest child, you need Garmond. He will care for you and protect you, long after I have gone on to the quiet lands to rest," Rora Moss said, gently smoothing Fintray's hair from her eyes.

"No!" Fintray screamed, terrified. "You can't leave me. Mother, promise you won't leave me." Her struggles increased and Garmond was having a harder time holding her in place. Her fear and her strong magic would soon overpower even his ability to hold her. He was sure something dreadful was about to occur and he had no way to stop it.

Rora Moss took Fintray's face in her hands and looked at her serenely. She explained softly, "Child, I can not promise that to you and would not if I could. It would be wrong for me to want to stay after the bargain I made with Garmond. The gods would prevent it and we would all suffer for it. It will be alright. Trust the gods to watch over you and know that I will be happy. One day you can join me there, in your own time." Her total comfort in her belief was not breaking through to her young daughter.

Fintray's terror was shifting to a great rage. She grabbed Garmond by the fur of his neck and forced him to stare into her eyes. "Is this true? Did you make this terrible bargain?" She shook him like a rag doll. "How could you do this to me? You are suppose to be my friend!"

Garmond looked at her calmly and said, "Wingling, you know it to be true, deep within yourself you know this. If it were not, you would not be so upset. Yes, with a stolen wish stone from the gods, your mother and I bargained. I used your soul in trade to her and have bonded myself to you to prevent the gods from sending me into darkness. Even if you hate me, it will not change the fact that we are bonded to each other. It will not change or diminish our responsibility to this place and these people." He was talking to her as calmly as he could, though his own fear and worry were growing.

As angry as she was, Fintray still loved Garmond and could not hurt him. "Garmond," she said in quiet talk, "who is my father?" This was not the question he was expecting and caught by surprise he had to tell her the truth.

Garmond hung his head and took a deep breath. "Fintray, my beloved Wingling, I am the soul that fathered you, in my previous form." He looked at her with deep love and longing in his eyes. "Part of the bargain I made was that I had to give up that form forever."

Fintray seemed to accept this without more distress, though it was hard to tell, because her panic was so very deep. Then she asked out loud, "Why am I so afraid? How can we fix this?" Her voice had a hard core of determination.

Garmond laid his head on her lap. "I'm sorry, Wingling, that is my fault as well. To make the bargain with your mother, I stole that wish stone from the gods, but I found that it could only be used in certain ways. They would allow the trade of souls, and the bonding which saved me from darkness, but the price was to take Rora Moss' fear of the sea and to give you two other greater fears. One you can fight with your magic, which is your fear of the wind."

"And the other?" Fintray asked, even though in her heart she knew the answer. He closed his eyes so he could not see her face when he told her.

"Being left by your mother," Garmond said. "I did not realise that this fear was as great as it is. I did not know that the gods would set such a high price on you. Believe me when I tell you that if I had known the hurt it would do you, I would never have risked any of it. I would have accepted being chained in darkness. I was selfish, just trying to save myself, before I knew you and loved you as I do. Forgive me, Wingling. I am so sorry." Tears leaked from the wolf's closed eyes.

Fintray collapsed into a fit of weeping, her tears mixing with his. For long minutes, nothing could quiet or comfort her.

Rora Moss shook her head sadly. Not knowing what else to do, she got up to put the kettle on and make some tea. Strathy, sitting on the hearth, held the baby quietly. The sorrow in the room was so heavy and so much of the joy of the day had been lost by all this emotion and none of them were sure of what to do.

Fintray rocked herself on the floor, hugging her knees to her chest. Tears washed down her face in rivers. Garmond licked them off her face and tried to reach her.

Strathy, trying to comfort her, said confidently, "Fintray, angel, don't fret. We will figure this out. Not to worry so. I am sure Balgavney can help, or the gods. All is not lost, dear child." He continued to rock the baby, holding her closely to his chest while patting Fintray on the shoulder.

Fintray looked over at him with eyes that were deep wells of hopelessness and he glanced up at Rora Moss concerned. The older woman stepped over to the kitchen hearth and set the kettle back on its hook. Hoping to comfort the young woman, she said matter-of-factly, "Enough, Fintray. We all must leave life and be left in our own time. This is not the end of the world. Pull yourself together." Rora Moss reasoned that being straight with the child would get through to her, not realising the true depth of her magically created fear.

Fintray leaped to her feet, suddenly vastly strong, and grabbed Garmond, shifting to her winged form at the same moment. Just as they had started to meld, she screamed, "It is the end of the world to me and I will not allow it. You will not leave me, ever!" Garmond pulled away in panic, trying to break her hold on him and prevent the melding, but her rage made her magic too strong.

There was a brief struggle as Garmond tried to fight her great power, but in the end the terror and anger was too much even for him, and their forms blended. The wolf-headed angel filled the room and begin to glow. Suddenly a voice that could be heard from the edge of the bay and the top of the hill cried out, "None of you will leave me. I won't have it."

In the blink of an eye, Strathy and the baby Cullerlie shifted into small white stones sitting by the fire place. Rora Moss became the same at the kitchen hearth. In an instant, in every house, every place, in the entire village, every last-life soul turned to stone, including my daughter.

She and I had been sitting by my fire, in my own comfortable house, having our tea and discussing the wise ways when I heard the great voice of the Wolf Angel and was afraid. My daughter looked confused for just an instant, then before my eyes, I watched my beloved Skirza turn to stone and wept because there was nothing I could do to stop or change it. All my wisdom and learning overcome in a moment of grief from a child, not even my own. I have never been so helpless in all my lives.

Kemnay remembers Trader

In the meadow, the memory of this ghastly night causes Balgavney to put her face into her hands and weep as if her heart were breaking. Once again, Kemnay tries to go to her and offer what comfort he can, but the barrier pushes him back. All he can do is sit and watch this beautiful woman cry before him. Clola wraps herself around him and offers what comfort she can. The wise woman's tears and sobs touch a deep place in both of them trapped helpless by the magic barrier.

After a few moments Balgavney's tears slow and she catches her breath. "I'm so sorry, Kemnay. I honestly had thought I could tell all this to you and not cry. Obviously I was very wrong. I will never forget the terrible sight of watching my daughter turn to stone before my eyes. Even after so many seasons, it still breaks my heart," the wise woman says with a sob, trying to slow her tears.

"Do not apologize," he says stiffly. "I can see that this has hurt you beyond words, as I know from my own experience." He feels clumsy in his attempt to comfort her, but it is all he can do. He knows he will have to deal with his own grief and sorrow to help here. This task gets harder for him every moment.

"Thank you for listening to me. I want to hear what you have experienced, but not tonight. Tonight, I must rest," Balgavney says, wiping her face with the edge of her skirts. She lifts her head, listening. "I hear Tifty coming with supper. We will have to talk more of this tomorrow. Please?" Her eyes are pleading with him to understand, and he answers as best he can.

"Of course. I will be glad for a meal. I feel as if I have been on the water for a year with nothing but dried meats, hollow as an old log," he says, looking towards the sea and seeing the sun beginning to set. Tifty comes over the hill with a basket and a blanket, and the children are with her. Their laughter is such a contrast to the deep feeling of sorrow that surrounds them.

Tifty takes one look at Balgavney's grieving face and puts a strong arm around her shoulder. She nods at Paddler to let him know not to worry, she will watch over the wise woman. He is grateful once again to this sensible woman. She tells the children, "Give Paddler that basket and blanket. I'm going to take Balgavney home now. I can see it has been a long day for the both of them. Be quick now." The children look at the adults with serious eyes.

Skene and Ythsie bring the things over to him and he thanks them gravely. He looks after the inn keeper, who is walking with her arm about Balgavney speaking softly. "Thank you," he calls softly after them. Tifty waves but otherwise concentrates her attention on the sad wise woman.

The children run after their mother and the wise woman, throwing him a concerned look. He picks up Clola and holds her to his chest for a moment, then sets her on his shoulder, takes the basket and blanket, and trudges back down along the river to his camp as the light fades out of the sky. He has much to think about and many questions to ask, but now he is hungry and tired, and wants only food, his fire and his bed.

Before he leaves the river, he fills his water skin. The clear water looks very inviting to him. He looks at the sky and sees he has enough daylight left for a bath. He returns to his camp, sets the basket aside, and throws the blanket onto his bed roll. He digs through his pack and finds a small chunk of soap. Taking a clean tunic, he walks through the quiet of the evening to the river, strips off his clothing and throws himself into the cold water. Clola joins him and he scrubs her scales until she shines in the dying light.

He stands quietly watching the water, deeply thoughtful, just letting Balgavney's story settle in his mind. He stretches and wants only to attend to the needs of his body for the moment and give his mind a rest.

As he shakes off the water and puts dry clothing on, Clola asks him, "You understand what has happened here, don't you?" The dragon knows the man is avoiding the situation, as he has for long years, but the time has come when he must face it and himself. She is not sure he is ready, but that doesn't matter. They are trapped here until they solve it. She wants to overcome the problem here so that they can continue with their travels, not spend eternity in a dead-end loop here.

"I've a pretty good idea," Kemnay replies with a sigh. "For now, I think I shall see if Tifty's basket is as wonderful tonight as the others have been." He takes a moment to band his wet hair behind his neck.

Clola prefers he leave it down, but knows he won't while it is wet, until he is back by the fire where it will dry.

Kemnay gathers the soap and clothing, and walks back to camp, preoccupied. He doesn't stop to pick up Clola, who has been sunning herself on a warm rock, so she just flies after him. She does make sure to bump him on the shoulder, several times on the way down the path, he bats at her absently. Unless she starts another fight with him, he is going to be moody and she would rather eat than fight. There will be time later to remind him not to ignore her.

Back at camp, Kemnay puts away his soap and sets things in order. He stirs up the fire, adding more fuel, then fills his cooking pot with water and sets it next to the fire to boil some for tea. He checks his boat and finds a small bit of moisture on the inside, so he carefully tips it from side to side to get the sea water to drain and then dries it with his dirty shirt. Keeping his boat in good repair is important, though he doubts he will use it again any time soon. He may go out just for the exercise. Looking at the sea cliffs and the sun nearly gone from the sky, he decided that tonight would not be a good time for that. The bay is still, but he is unfamiliar with the pattern of the tides and hidden rocks. Perhaps in the morning, to help settle his emotions. Being in the boat helps him to think and keeps him fit as well.

He returns to the fire to find the water boiling, so he carefully puts some leaves in his battered cup and pours the hot water over them, then sets them aside to brew. He reaches for the basket Tifty has provided, ready to explore the wonders of what she has brought him. Clola is watching with interest as well.

Tonight there is a fish pie with potatoes and strong cheese melted on top, another joint of beef, more bread, butter and jam, some vegetables, which he tosses into his still-steaming pot to boil, more porridge grain, sugar and milk, and some fat sausages as well. At the bottom are some sweet pastries and a flask of wine. He sets the breakfast things back in the basket and places the rest by the fire. Looking at the wine flask, he sets it aside, but still within easy reach.

He asks Clola what she would like. The dragon offers to share the fish pie and the beef joint or just leave him to starve, for being so difficult. His eyes show a ghost of a smile and he says, "Go ahead little one. I am not sure I am hungry. Perhaps I'll just have the wine and skip the food." He reaches for the flask and she shifts larger to block his hand.

"Oh no you don't," she says warningly, her jewelled eyes glowing in the firelight. "First you have food, and we talk, then you can have the wine. Wine puts you to sleep and makes you grouchy in the morning, especially if you skip food. I'll not have you ruin my breakfast because of a hangover." She bats the flask out of his reach.

He laughs at her and takes some of the meat off the joint and some of the fish pie as well. She shifts smaller again and attacks the rest of the fish pie with gusto, then finishes off the beef, bones and all. He has some of the bread, butter and jam and offers her some, but she burps and refuses. She is content and ready to talk.

Looking up at him from beside the fire, she asks, "Did you find another pumpkin?" She already knows the answer, as they had been together all day, but she can't help teasing him a little, so she also continues, ignoring his look of annoyance at her. "I'd like one for breakfast."

He shakes his head, and sighs. "You know I didn't bring one down. It will be porridge, eggs, sausages and whatever we have from Tifty. You shouldn't be so greedy." He drinks his tea slowly. "Besides, I'm rather concerned you will turn into a pumpkin one of these days, or at least start turning orange."

To oblige him, she shifts her scales to a bright pumpkin colour over her full belly. This makes him laugh. "See, I told you," he chortles. She sticks her tongue out at him.

The dragon relaxes back to her normal green; no need to waste energy shifting when there is no danger, after all. With another burp, she heaves herself to her feet and walks over to sit on his lap. He has not reached for the wine, a rare treat for him and tends to make him relaxed and silly. This is fine with her, but she knows he is thinking that it might be a relief after such a long day. Later it will not be a problem, but for the moment she needs all of his attention.

He sits staring at the fire and strokes her smooth scales absently. He is thinking about what Balgavney has said. He wonders if the pair Fintray and Garmond have returned to the statue, but he is not convinced of it. Although the magic at the image was strong, there was a definite air of emptiness there. They had to be somewhere nearby, but the question was where, and in what form? The shock and grief Balgavney spoke of, and showed, was great. It is possible that even now it would feel like a fresh wound. He wondered if Fintray had realised the hurt she had done to the people she loved so much.

He remembers his own village and flinches. Clola bites him gently on the hand to get his attention turned to her. "Don't go off in a funk now," she orders. "There will be time for that another day." She settles again, knowing he would be within easy reach of her sharp teeth. It isn't the nicest way to get someone's attention, but it is rather effective.

Kemnay drains the rest of his tea and set the cup aside. He would have some of the wine later, but he needs a clear head for this. "We know Garmond, don't we, Little One?" There was anger in his voice. It is ironic that the man who managed to pull Paddler back to reality was banished from it himself.

"Yes, we do, which should be to our advantage, for now we have his true name," Clola says, resting her chin on her claws. She is thoughtful and reaches out with her mind to the universe, looking for answers. Now that she has questions and some reminders, she should be able to access the information that will help them.

"We met Garmond at the village before we left the last time. He was a trader, who said he came from the gods." She was picking up speed in the review of her memory. "He carried threads and cloth, and I remember that he was a very moody fellow."

Kemnay nods in agreement. "He was that. I remember sitting with him at the inn one night. He threw cups across the room and then in an instant was buying a round for everyone. The inn keeper was quite afraid of him."

Clola replies, "A lot of folks were afraid of him. Remember the only people he could always get along with were Merry and you. He used to sleep in her back room. She told me once he was a touched god-child who was searching for an answer." The dragon was very thoughtful.

"Yes, I remember now." Kemnay responds, feeling more confident. "I sat late one night with him, by the fire, and he told me he was on a quest to free himself from the gods. He looked at me and told me he felt that one day I would help him escape them. Of course I agreed. His moods were too changeable and he seemed in such great need." He nods to himself thoughtfully. "I didn't know his name then. He was just Trader, or when he wasn't around, Mad Trader."

"So the promise was made before we arrived here and that makes it doubly important to help and heal," Clola says firmly. "It may help us to find the lost as well."

For a moment, Kemnay is silent. "Oh, Little One, this is so hard, but if I can fix this, I'll be able to help Merry. I'm afraid she is living the life that Balgavney is living, trapped in the same incarnation." A look of pain crosses his face. "I didn't know what I was doing. All my life I was only talking to stones and exploring. It happened so quickly and I was so frightened."

Clola touches him gently and says softly, "You did not do intentional harm. Yes, in a small way, it was still harm, but you will be able to change it, because there is no malice or rage involved. This place has a much bigger problem. It is also possible that what you did is different because of how it happened."

"I can only hope," he says sadly. "The thought that I have trapped Merry and the good people of our village for all time is hard for me." The memory makes him wince.

"I don't believe it is the same at all," Clola says calmly. "For one thing, the village was still active and the only souls you turned to stone were your parents, not the entire village. You and Merry moved their stone to the village circle, and I am sure they can be restored. You are the only direct link left to them."

Paddler looked stricken. "Do you suppose Merry is still waiting for me? Oh, Clola, it has been so very long. Have I trapped her too?" His voice was breaking, so he paused for a moment and took a breath. "You are right, it was different. The village was still there and there was a birth before we left, and two of the oldsters passed on. Here, things seem to be frozen, and the village is abandoned as well. Ours was not -- it was still doing well when we left." This thought reassures the troubled man.

He sits staring into the fire, adding fuel every so often to keep the blaze high. She allows him to search his memory. What he needs to know is in there, and given time and quiet he will be able to reach it. She looks at him softly and gives the silent command, "Remember," then sets her chin on her claws and silently follows the paths his mind takes.

Kemnay remembers well the night he turned his own parents to stone. It is unlikely, no matter how long he lives, that he would forget that. The memory is like a firebrand in his brain. But the days that followed were strange as well.

Kindness of Achath

The morning after he had lost his parents, Achath came by with a basket of food. She was one of the few in the village that used her true name. She was not afraid of being magically hurt as Merry was, sadly. This would seem to be her unmaking and cause a great hurt to Paddler and the others in the village. She was a lovely woman with chestnut hair and bright blue eyes, but only truly special when she smiled.

Achath went in and put her basket on the table, next to the others brought by the village folks. She stirred up his fire and added fuel to it, looked in on him, then sat in the chair by the fire, sewing quietly, waiting for him to wake. After talking late into the night with Merry, she was reassured that he would be all right. At the critical time he had done what needed to be done, despite his broken heart. She cared deeply for this man, even though he was older than she. If he had been aware enough to notice, he would have seen the love in her eyes. She was worried about him. She would have been happy to be a wife to him and love his dragon as well, but she knew the gods had great plans for him that would involve him leaving the village, and she was needed here. Achath kept her love to herself, but she could not abandon him on such a sad day as this.

Clola heard the woman come in, opened an eye and watched her from the bed. She understood the young woman's feelings, and admired her quiet acceptance, though sometimes she was annoyed with Paddler for not noticing the woman. Achath was a good cook, and Clola appreciated that. She also wasn't at all upset by the dragon's temperament or behaviour, which was definitely in her favour. As the woman sat sewing, the dragon yawned and slid off the edge of the bed. The man was still in the deep sleep of grief and exhaustion, but the dragon was hungry. She wandered out to the young wise woman and bumped her on the elbow with her forehead to get her attention. The young woman smiled down at the small creature.

Achath said softly, "Hello, Little One. Are you hungry?" There were many baskets of food, for even as she waited more of the villagers came in with silent offerings for the young man and his companion. All were careful not to disturb his rest.

Clola replied, "Of course I am hungry. I am always hungry, and he made me hunt my own supper last night." She jumped up on the table and stuck her nose in to a nearby basket, nearly knocking another off, impatient as always when food was available.

Achath laughed quietly, so as not to disturb Paddler. "Get down from there, Little One. I will see what there is and give you a meal. You need not make a mess of the whole thing." The young woman set her sewing aside and walked over, picking the dragon up off the table and setting the small creature on her shoulder. She was one of the few humans beside Paddler that could carry the dragon. The young woman began searching through the baskets and setting food on the small hearth for the dragon.

"I don't suppose there is any pumpkin?" Clola said plaintively. She felt a moment's sadness for the loss of Weaver, who made the best pumpkin stew in the village. It was sad to know she would never have it again. In her own way, she felt the grief that Paddler had, as well as her own, but she also saw the greater turn of the wheel. What made her the most sad was that his parents would be kept from the quiet lands.

Every basket had something in it with pumpkin, as all the village knew of the small dragon's love for the bright fruit. It was a feast fit for a hungry dragon. After assembling the meal for Little One on the hearth, Achath set the kettle on the fire and put various leaves in a mug to make a healing tea. She knew that sleep was needed for healing, but so was food. She would brew the tea and then go to wake Paddler.

Clola looked up from her feast, hearing the wise woman's thought and offered to wake him with a good hard bite to his backside. Achath told her to just eat and give the poor man a break from being chewed on this day. Clola reluctantly agreed, though she said, "It would serve him right after the mess he nearly made."

Achath said sternly, "Hush now. It was accidental and no harm will come of it. He needs no more hurt from you. His own hurt is more than enough."

Admonished, the dragon returned to her food and decided to behave. This woman was feeding her willingly and that was something to encourage. What Paddler had never learned that both his mother and this young woman had was that the dragon was very aware of motivated self interest and feeding her was the best way to get her to behave. Paddler knew she could feed herself and often let her, much to her annoyance. It wasn't the broom that kept her in line but the tasty food, lovingly offered.

After a short time, Achath had a strong cup of healing tea ready, and she walked over and sat on the edge of Paddler's bed. She set the mug on the table beside the bed, under the window. The sun shone on Paddler's face, which was drawn with pain and above it, his hair was in disorder. For a moment she just looked at him, her heart brimming with unspoken feelings. Gently, she reached out a hand and smoothed his brow, calling his name softly.

"Paddler, you must wake now. Come, my friend, I have tea and food for you." She took his shoulder gently and gave him a small shake.

He turned his head to his pillow and muttered, "Go away, I am not hungry." He did not want to wake to the reality of his loss from the comfort of his dreams. He tried to pull the blanket over his head, but since he was on top of it, was unsuccessful. He blinked up at Achath, like an owl in daylight. She smiled down at him.

She waited patiently, as she knew he was slow to wake on a good day, which today was not. The only time he woke quickly was if there was danger or if Little One tormented him. She lifted the mug of tea from the table, put her hand behind his shoulder and helped him to sit. He took a sip from the offered mug and finding it a comfortable temperature, he took a larger swallow. She smiled at him and got up, returning to the kitchen table to set out a meal for him. He sat on the edge of the bed, clutching the tea mug in both hands, watching her move around his home.

After a few moments he realised the woman was not going to give up or go away until he ate. He excused himself and went out to his privy, relieved himself, then took a moment to splash water on his face and look up the road to where his parents' house sat. Slowly, he went back into the house and sat down to have the meal Achath placed before him. He didn't remember what he ate, but he was grateful for the gentle kindness of this good woman. It was a healing balm to his broken heart.

When he finished, he sat by the fire, stroking Clola absently. She was laid out and content, burping as usual. Achath cleaned up from the meal and organised the remaining food so that it would be easy for them to feed themselves later after she had left. She then sat down and picked up her sewing again.

Softly, she asked, "Paddler, would you like me to help you settle your parents' home?" She was holding her breath, unsure of how he would respond to this.

He looked startled at her question, as he had been drifting in the nameless pain he had no words for and her question jarred him back to the reality of the situation. He cannot leave their home to moulder; it must be made ready for someone else. His mother's loom must be righted and put away, his father's tools given to someone to make good use of. The weight of having to go back there and touch what they had left was great indeed, and his tears began to flow again. She looked at him, compassion shinning from her blue eyes and said, "I know this hurts, but it will be alright. Merry is sure that they are happy. You have done no great harm." Her own eyes brimmed with tears of shared sorrow.

"How can we be sure?" he said with an empty heart. "After what I have done, why have I not been chased out of the village with anger?" His guilt was so deep that he was battling himself, fully expecting the others around him to do the same. He suddenly realised that the kitchen was all but overflowing with food and his friend was sitting and watching him quietly. If it was as terrible as he believed, surely this would not be the case. A small candle flame of hope started to help him reach into his grief.

Achath looked at him, familiar with grief, shaking her head. "Silly man, we all feel such anger and hurt when those we love pass on. It is only that it happened so suddenly that is making it harder for you. Trust me, there are none in the village that hold you responsible. Nothing terrible has happened." She patted his arm soothingly, wishing she had the courage to take him in her arms and mix her tears with his, but he was too vulnerable right now and would not understand. His destiny was so different from hers, but it didn't stop the wanting in her heart.

"Thank you, Achath," he said. "You are a good friend to me." For a moment his hand covered hers. Her love shone from her gentle eyes, but was missed by his grieving ones. He sighed. "I suppose I shall have to go up there, but not today. I am so very tired." He looked ready to return to his bed.

Achath said softly, "Go back to sleep, my friend. I will return later and make sure you eat again, and I will sit here tonight so you will not be alone. Tomorrow we can go up to the house. It will be all right to leave it until then." She took his hand, led him back to his bed, pulled back the covers so he could be under them and kissed him on the forehead like a child. He instantly fell back to sleep.

"Little One," the wise woman said, "come for me if he wakes. I am going to care for Merry now and I will return later. Be nice." She shook a finger at the dragon dozing by the fire. Clola, in her usual way, stuck out her tongue at Achath but agreed to her demands.

Achath left her sewing in the basket, by the chair at the fire. She didn't expect to sleep that night, so it was good she had much to keep her hands busy. With a lighter heart, she returned to Merry's house to fix a meal for her and tell the older woman what was happening with the bonded pair. They talked into the afternoon, and after Merry had supper, Achath returned to the workshop to wake Paddler for another meal. She would let him sleep this night, but tomorrow she was going to force him to go outdoors and move around. Rest was important for grief, but motion was needed for healing.

Early the next morning, Paddler woke with one arm numb, because Clola was laying on it and the circulation had stopped. He tried to pull it from under her without disturbing her, but she turned her face to his shoulder and bit him. He pushed her out of the bed and she landed on the floor with a thud. He grabbed the blanket and before she could launch herself at him, he tossed it over her and made for the door.

He paused for a moment when he saw Achath sleeping in the chair by the fire. There was a shaft of morning sunlight on her hair and she looked very peaceful. He was grateful to her. Behind him, he heard Clola freeing herself from the blanket and he rushed out the door to the privy. If they were going to have a fight, he would rather not disturb his friend's sleep. Clola came flying up behind him and he shut the door in her face at the last moment, so that she bashed into it.

After he finished he opened the door cautiously and looked for the dragon. She wasn't in his line of sight so he assumed she had gone off for some breakfast. What he forgot to check was the roof overhead. He was halfway back to the house when he heard her take flight behind him. He knew he couldn't outrun her, but still tried. She hit him between the shoulder blades just as he got to the front door and knocked him over. He landed with a great clattering thud, which woke Achath. The wise woman started to laugh as she saw the two of them wrestling on the floor, but was concerned that they would break things.

She said loudly, "Stop it, you two! If you want to fight, do so outside. How can I fix breakfast with the two of you underfoot?" Her voice was stern, but her eyes were laughing.

Clola flew up to her shoulder and said crossly, "He threw me out of bed and slammed the door in my face. He doesn't deserve any breakfast." The dragon made as if to launch herself onto the table.

Achath grabbed her and cradled her in her arm like a small child. She said quietly, "I am sorry he treated you so badly, Little One, but I will still fix him breakfast. If it makes you feel better, I won't share any of the pumpkin with him."

"Now wait a minute here," Paddler shouted. "She was sleeping on my arm and it was numb. I was only trying to move her gently and she bit me." He managed to get himself off the floor and looked ready to pounce on the young woman to get at the dragon.

The young woman held her hand up to him to stop him. "Hush now, there is plenty for all of us. Go make your bed and I'll fix food and tea." She moved the dragon up to her shoulder and started moving around the kitchen. Once again, Paddler had lost the argument and with bad grace, like a spoiled child, he stomped into the other room.

Achath called after him, suppressing a giggle. "You might want to change your clothes as well, since you've slept in those for two days." His reply was muffled and she suspected that she probably didn't want to hear it any way. She smiled and set the dragon on the hearth with a large plate of food.

He returned in clean clothing and sat at the table. The young woman set a plate down and joined him with one of her own. He frowned at her and then at the dragon, who he noticed was halfway through her own meal. Realising he wouldn't get his own if he didn't hurry, he quickly ate the food before him. Clola finished and crawled up on his lap, fighting him for the last of his food. Achath just laughed.

Later, they went up to the home of his parents together. It was hard for the man, but the quiet support of the young woman got him though it. He managed to find people who could use most of what was left, kept a few things for himself and gave the place a good cleaning. There was a newly married couple in the village that would be glad of a home of their own, since they were still living with the bride's parents.

For the next few weeks, Achath made a point of visiting him every day and helping to keep his spirits up. He returned to his workshop and would often come into his rooms in the evening to find her waiting with a meal ready for them. He was grateful for her kindness and was starting to notice how happy he was when she was around.

Paddler and Achath

One evening, when the young woman was busy delivering a baby, he went to the inn for a meal. There he met the one called Trader to his face and Mad Trader out of hearing, who asked after his mother. Paddler explained that his parents were gone. Trader asked when that happened.

Paddler got each of them a mug of ale and sat by the fire to talk with the man, thinking he would be one more person who would have good memories of his parents to share. He remembered that his mother had often gotten threads from Trader, though she wouldn't allow him into the house, and always met him at the inn.

Trader again asked what happened, and said that he had heard rumours that it was sudden. He implied that he thought the young man had been at fault. Paddler explained as well as he could that he had turned them to stone. The deranged man's face looked shocked, except for his eyes, which shone with a dark hope.

"You turned them to stone? What a cruel thing for you to have done. Now they can never reach the quiet lands. I'm surprised they didn't banish you from the village for that," Trader said unkindly.

Paddler choked on his ale. "What do you mean?" he asked, with his guilt rising in his heart again. Despite Merry and Achath's continued assurance, he was never sure if what he had done was right. "I didn't do it intentionally. It was an accident."

Trader went on, "It is no accident to use your great power to call on the gods and make them answer. I know the gods. When they are forced do such as that the cost is dear. Very dear indeed. Do you have a wife or a lover or a child you are ready to trade to them to save your own skin?" His voice grated on Paddler's nerves.

"I have no one. My parents were all my family," said Paddler sadly. "Only my companion is left, and if the gods wanted to take her, I couldn't stop them." He was very sorry he had sat with the mad man now.

"Ah, you are protected by her, then," Trader said slyly. "If I could have such a companion, that would keep me away from their notice for all time." He reached his hand towards Clola, who hissed at him and changed her colour to a warning red. He quickly pulled his hand away. "No offence, Little One, just what I know of the gods."

Paddler excused himself and went home, troubled by the strange man's words and the worries in his heart.

The next day, Paddler was busy in his workshop when he felt a presence behind him. Clola hissed a warning, and he turned suddenly with a hammer in his hand to find Trader standing in his doorway. For a moment the boat builder held it threateningly, but soon set it aside and asked curtly, "What do you want?"

Today, Trader was all niceness and smiles. "Paddler, during the night my boat came untied and drifted into the rocks and was damaged. I was hoping you might look at her. I want to be gone before the season of storms, but don't really want to take the chance of sinking. I know you are the best boat maker in all the isles. Will you look at her for me?" The trader's voice was reasonable and calm.

Paddler could not refuse the man's cry for help, so he set his tools in their places and walked to the waterside with Trader, listening to the strange man talk lightly about the places he was going and the cargo he had. On the far side of the bay was the boat, caught on the beach rocks. The Trader had managed to get the boat out of the water and the damage was not too serious, but it was enough to make taking a long trip a concern. Paddler looked at the underside and found a place where a rock had weakened a plank, but he felt that a patch would hold until it was time to bring the boat up for the winter. There was also a place on the keel that looked to have taken some damage. He told Trader that he could fix the boat in a few days.

Paddler put a temporary patch of pitch and tar over the outside weak plank so she would not sink and they managed to get her refloated at high tide without doing more damage to her. They floated her to Paddler's working dock and set her in a frame that could be pulled above the water so that she could be repaired. There was a crack in the keel, which he filled with resins. He warned the trader that the repairs would only be temporary, and if he hit any rocks again it would most likely be the end of the boat. It was old and battered from wear and was in serious need of an overhaul.

Trader was grateful for the young man's help and during the three days he stayed, he was good company and spoke only kind words. Merry came by when she saw his boat and talked to him. The crazed man was humble before the wise woman and always had a gift for her. Achath came by to tell Paddler about the birth of the new babe. It was her first actual meeting with the Trader, though she knew of him. She seemed cautious around him, but soon warmed to his talk, though she would not accept a gift from his hands or touch him. Unusually, when Achath was near Trader, Clola sat on her shoulder, hissing softly if the man came too close.

The boat was repaired in good time and Trader had decided to leave on the morning tide. He offered to take Paddler to the inn for ale. As Paddler was putting away the tools, Merry came to the door and invited the two men to join her and Achath for supper. She also told Trader that he could have her back room for the night, to enjoy a last sleep in a good bed before he was again on his boat. The dark man thanked her gravely and accepted. It seemed that Achath was sitting with one of the village oldsters who was dying, and could not join them. Paddler was disappointed, as he had come to enjoy the young woman's company very much, but was also relieved to have her away from Trader's calculating looks.

The meal was genial and Paddler bid the wise woman and the trader good night. He stepped into the darkness and was walking quietly by the shore when he found Achath sitting on a stone by the water's edge. He walked up to her and said, "Hello, Achath. I thought you were sitting with the oldster tonight?" She looked startled for a moment, even frightened until she realised it was her friend.

"Hello, Paddler," she said. "I have been sitting with him, but his children wanted some time to say good-bye to him, so I have left them for a short while and come to rest and watch the water. It is so beautiful." She pointed to the clear water lapping gently at her feet.

He sat on the stone beside her and she shifted slightly so that their hips touched. "It is beautiful," the young man said, and added shyly, "but so are you."

She smiled. "Good of you to notice," she whispered, feeling Clola bump her with her forehead. She raised her voice and said, "Thank you, Paddler, that is very kind." She leaned her weight slightly towards the man.

He was thinking about this lovely woman sitting beside him, how much her kindness had helped him since the death of his parents, how much his mother and father had liked her. One thought led to another and he slowly put his arm around her shoulder.

Speaking softly, he said, "Achath, you are a very good friend to me. I think a better friend than I deserve at times."

He leaned down to kiss her on the cheek and she turned her head slightly so that the soft kiss was on her lips instead. For a moment the man was startled, but then relaxed and enjoyed the brief contact.

Behind them they heard a giggle and a child's voice going, "Oh, mushy stuff." One of the oldster's grandchildren had come looking for the wise woman and caught her kissing the boat maker. He couldn't wait to tell the whole village.

Achath quickly stood up and patted her skirts. "Child," she said sternly, "you had no need to spy on me. You only had to call my name and I would come. Good night, Paddler." She smiled at the man and, for a moment, laid her warm hand on his face. "I will talk to you tomorrow." She waved farewell.

Paddler was warmed by the brief kiss and a little startled as well. He was beginning to understand that Achath had feelings for him that he hadn't noticed. He put his hand to his lips and felt her warmth there. He glanced towards her walking with the child. Feeling his eyes on her, she turned and smiled, lifting a hand to him before going into the house to tend the dying man. It was the last time Paddler saw her.

Paddler was walking home in a very distracted frame of mind. Even Clola's hiss and bite on his shoulder didn't attract his attention. He was speculating about Achath and wondering if she might be willing to make a home with him. All dreams of travelling were pushed aside and the idea of living his life building boats and having a family with her was strong.

Achath missing

Clola was restless and worried. She had felt the presence of the Mad Trader and did not trust him. She was sure he could not hurt Paddler, but she was not sure of what other mischief he might cause. After Paddler slipped to sleep, she quietly let herself out of the house and went to talk to Merry.

Merry answered her rattling at the door, slightly sleepy. She had been dozing in her chair. She told Clola that Trader had stopped by earlier to tell her he would feel better sleeping on his boat and didn't want to disturb her leaving for the early tide. Clola was both relieved and troubled that the man was not close by.

Clola asked Merry, "Why is he so different all the time? I don't like the way he feels. I think he means harm." Clola was worried about Paddler.

Merry replied in a sad voice, "Little One, he has been touched by the gods. I don't know if he got too close out of mischief or misadventure, but sometimes his mind is muddled by them. I am sure it hurts him. He is only a lost, troubled soul in need of kindness." The old woman did her best to reassure the dragon.

The small creature was not convinced. "I suspect he has some mischief of his own planned. It is odd to me that someone who lives so often with boats would allow his to come untied and be damaged," the dragon said skeptically, referring to the damage that Paddler had just repaired.

Merry shook her finger at the dragon and scolded, "What a doubtful creature you are. One who is so much mischief herself has little room to talk. Even the most experienced of boatmen can be tired and miss a loop of a knot. Ropes get old and break. Do not suspect unless you are sure." The old woman softened her scolding by stroking the scales of the dragon's forehead.

"Merry, I am worried," Clola said, looking out the dark window. "I feel like something terrible is going to happen."

Merry shook her head and went into her kitchen. "Little One, you must know most folks don't like the Mad Trader, as they feel his strangeness and don't trust it. He is not evil, just confused. Tomorrow he will be gone and then there will be nothing interesting going on in the village." The wise woman's voice held a laugh. "Well, at least until you start another fight with Paddler in the inn. If you keep it up the inn keeper will not allow you to return."

The dragon looked disgruntled. "All the better. I hate the smell of ale and the inn reeks of it. Worse, Paddler actually drinks the stuff and then smells of it."

Merry laughed at the small creature and her disgust and walked over, offering her a bite of pumpkin candy. It was a favourite treat of the small creature and could usually cheer her up. Clola brightened when she saw what Merry was holding and opened her mouth wide so the wise woman could drop the candy in. "Thank you, Merry," she said, chewing contentedly.

"You are welcome, Little One," Merry said, smiling. "Now go home and curl up with Paddler. Don't worry so much." The old woman walked to open the door so the small dragon could leave.

"Only one tiny piece?" Clola pouted, shifting her form slightly smaller so that her eyes looked large and pitiful. This was a trick she had learned that usually worked well for her.

Merry reached into a pocket and pulled out two more pieces. "Here, you greedy creature, now get you to your bed," the wise woman said, offering the treat to the gleeful dragon. Clola snatched it and scampered out the door. Merry laughed and went to her own bed with an untroubled heart.

The dragon, delighted with her treat, went home and curled up on the bed by Paddler, burping softly. She went to sleep feeling reassured by her talk with Merry, but she would be very glad to know that the Trader was gone.

Clola woke just after dawn, feeling that something was wrong. It lasted only for an instant, then the feeling faded. She looked around the house, found nothing out of place, and decided she was just tired and curled up by Paddler, then went back to sleep. Paddler's sleep was undisturbed.

No one saw Achath get on the Trader's boat, nor did anyone see him leave. In the morning his boat was gone, much to the relief of most of the village. No one suspected what he had done and even later it was only speculation. The village did occasionally have raiders, but it was rare indeed for anyone to harm a wise woman. For a long time there was no connection made between the mad trader's leaving and the missing wise woman.

It was not until later in the day that Merry raised the alarm. The old woman found that Achath was missing when she went into the younger one's room and found her bed had not been slept in. The wise woman walked to the oldsters house, surprised to find that he had died before dawn and the young woman had left. A search of the village path found only her scarf, caught on a tree limb, but no sign of the young woman. Paddler was especially frantic to find her, afraid his advances of the night before had made her leave.

Clola shifted to her great white dragon form and searched the nearby sea, but no sign could be seen of any boat in the area near the islands. The dragon also searched the hills, thinking perhaps the young woman had gone walking, but no sign was found of the young wise woman. Merry was especially sad at her loss, as she was feeling her age and afraid the village would be left without a wise woman to care for them. She didn't know what to do, and pleaded with the gods to protect the young woman.

After a few days, boats were sent out to the nearby isles to spread the word about the missing young woman. No sign of her was found and it remained a great mystery.

Paddler sat by Merry's fire one evening a few nights later, feeling especially downhearted. He confessed to Merry, "The night she disappeared I talked to her. We were sitting on the rocks." His voice held a deep guilt. "It is my fault Merry, I frightened her away."

The old woman's brow furrowed. "What are you talking about, child? How could you have frightened her? She loved you." The wise woman's voice was sharp with worry.

"Loved me as a friend, perhaps," Paddler said, "but I kissed her. I meant it only as a friend, but her face turned and I kissed her lips. It was an accident." He sounded so much younger than his years. His experience with women had been so limited because of living with a dragon companion.

Merry rolled her eyes and whispered, "Men are so stupid." Clola, laying at her feet, snorted softly. The wise woman kicked at the dragon lightly to keep her quiet.

The old wise woman stood up, walked over and took the young man's face in her hands. She looked into his eyes making sure his full attention was focused on her.

Speaking as she would to a difficult or slow child, she said deliberately, "Man-child, that woman loved you and would not have found your kiss unwanted. Besides, only in very rare circumstance can a wise woman be forced to do anything she is not willing to do. We are strongly protected by the gods and have strong magic of our own. You could not have kissed her if she was not willing. Open your stupid eyes and see that." Merry frowned at Paddler.

A light of hope crossed the man's eyes and again the wise woman rolled her own. He said, "Is this true, Merry? Could she really love me?"

Merry shook her head and went back to her chair. "Yes, of course it is true, you stupid man. She has loved you for many years, and if you had just opened your eyes you would have seen it." Merry stared into the fire, wondering what had become of the young woman and if somehow this man had something to do with it.

Paddler was awash in a wonder of mixed emotions. To find out that Achath loved him as more than a friend opened his eyes to her, but now she was missing. He had to do something.

"Merry," he asked, "is there not a way we can trace her with our magic? There has to be something we can do rather than just wait." The hope in his eyes lifted the old wise woman's spirits.

"Yes, child," the wise woman answered. "Tomorrow we will go to the magic circle and ask the gods directly if they will help us find her. I don't know if they will answer, but we can at least try." She rose tiredly from her chair and pointed to the door. "But enough for tonight, Paddler. I am tired and my old bones need rest."

He took her hint, kissed her lightly on the cheek, picked up Clola and went to his own bed.

Questioning the gods

At dawn the old wise woman tapped on his door, waking him and his companion. He dressed quickly and the three of them went to the magic circle together. Merry wanted to do the search before the rest of the village awoke for the day. She was not sure what the results might be and was keen to protect her village. The grasses were still damp and the air was cool. Paddler could tell it would soon be the season of the storms.

Merry walked into the circle with Paddler and Little One. Once inside, Clola shifted to be the same size as the two people. They stood in the centre of the circle, then held hands and claws to form an inner circle.

Merry whispered, "To the gods of the earth, sky and sea, we ask you to attend and assist us."

She looked at Paddler who nodded, and to Clola who did the same and then continued. "I, the wise woman Balmedie and the Bonded Pair of Kemnay and Clola call you to our aid for the finding of the wise woman Achath. She is missing from our village. We ask your help to find her, for she is dear to us." For several moments all was quiet.

On the ground inside their circle a pool of mist formed, made of dust, air and water. The gods at least were listening to them. The mist grew larger, and it formed three faces, one looking towards each of them.

To Merry, showing a face of stone, it spoke first. "Balmedie, I come to you. This young wise woman is lost to you, and you will have another to train before you are allowed to go on to your next rebirth. She will arrive by sea, soon." The wise woman nodded that she understood, but her heart was heavy with the news.

To Paddler, a face of water, the sea goddess, appeared. "Beloved Kemnay, the woman Achath is on the sea and you must search for her. Know that she is safe, but grieved. It will take you many years to find her and a great struggle within yourself and with others. You must find the one called Trader to help your search, but be warned he will not make it easy for you."

Kemnay accepted this and felt the first stirring of anger in his heart. The watery face before him looked stern and continued, "You must not lose hope, even if the search is long, nor must you let hate fill you. It is your task to heal suffering, even in those who do much harm. Do not lose sight of this task. It will be your undoing if you do not love all creatures, even those who seem least worthy of it." Kemnay nodded and let the anger go. He knew the power of love was the strongest of all and if he lost that, he would lose everything.

The face nearest Clola was a feathered one. "Companion Clola, you must guard this man and guide him. You can do much to help find this woman, if you learn to listen for her. Be ready always to keep him safe. Remember mischief can often cover a deeper intent." The face winked at Clola as the dragon nodded.

The three faces spoke at once. "Kemnay, you must take Clola and began the search for Achath. There will be many challenges along the way and the search will be long. Do not lose hope or sight of your goal. Balmedie you must be left behind to protect this place and these people. One will be sent who has the knowledge you need and then you will be released so that your training will not be broken. Clola, be ready."

The form was starting to dissolve before them, and with a last whisper it said, "The gods watch over all of you, do not be afraid." Then it was gone.

Balmedie stood with tears on her face. She was grieved to know the woman Achath had been lost and that her own journey would be so much longer. The old wise woman was ready for a rest, but the gods demand service and their rewards are few for those who succeed and none for those who fail. She would do what was needed. Merry was also sad to know that this young man whom she had spent so many years teaching and loving would go away, most likely to never be seen again.

Kemnay was in turmoil. He now suspected that Trader had taken Achath, but couldn't figure out how. With her protections the mad man could not have overpowered her. Somehow he must have tricked her, but even that would not have been an easy thing to do. Paddler would spend long hours wondering over her fate and how it had come to happen. Today he would load his travelling boat and go after them. He was strong and the sea was his friend, so he was sure he could catch them soon, despite the warnings from the gods of long travels.

Clola shifted back to her usual size and flew up to Kemnay's shoulder. The man walked over to the old wise woman and hugged her to him.

"Merry, it seems I must now leave this place," he said to her gently. "It is funny -- I always expected to, but not so suddenly or for these reasons."

He felt Merry nod against his chest. He released her and reached out with a gentle hand to wipe the tears from her face. "Be of good heart, my friend. I am sure the gods will watch over all of us." The love in his voice was strong.

Merry smiled sadly at Kemnay. "Yes, child, I expect things will work out. Never as I expect do the gods behave, but that is why they are gods and I am just an old wise woman."

She wiped her face off with the corner of her shawl and started out of the circle saying, "Well, before you go, I will fix you a good hot meal. I expect your Little One there is hungry."

Clola yawned from his shoulder. "Of course, we haven't had breakfast yet. Can't you see I am fading away?" For a moment she shifted smaller, then returned to her normal size. The two people laughed.

The three of them walked to Merry's home and she fed them well. Paddler went back and closed up the workshop, packed his gear and took his travelling boat to the water. As he paddled out of the bay he saw a passenger boat pull up and felt the presence of another wise woman. He mentally wished her well and started on his journey.

Balgavney and Kemnay compare stories

Paddler sits long past sunset, at his fire in the shelter of the trees wondering if he has finally found Achath, or if finding Garmond will at least give him the answers he needs to find her. He still remembers the touch of her lips that last time he saw her. He wonders if she remembers as well. Tomorrow, he will tell Balgavney what he knows. He is sure the wise woman here will be able to make sense of the situation.

The man looks deeply into the fire, which has long since burned to embers. He adds fuel and gets the fire going again, looks at the wine flask and sets it aside. He is tired enough that he doesn't need it to sleep. Holding the small dragon to his chest, he walks over to his bedroll and lays down. It is Achath's voice he has heard on the wind, her voice that helps him understand who at least the Mad Trader is. Tomorrow, he promises himself again, he will ask Balgavney if she has an idea to help. His tears blur his view of the firelight and Clola sings to him until he sleeps.

In the morning, after breakfast, Paddler goes up the hill to talk once again with Balgavney. He finds her waiting for him on the same stone as before, with a basket beside her feet. There is another by the stone he sits on. This morning, the wise woman's beautiful face is calm and her green eyes are shining. He feels rumpled and tired, as much of his sleep has been disturbed by dreams of the past.

"I greet you, Balgavney," he says in a rough voice. "We have much to talk about this day."

The wise woman smiles and replies, "I greet you as well, Kemnay and Clola. I agree there is much to talk about. I had Tifty make up lunch for us and the children helped me leave it for you. I thought it best if we were not interrupted this day." She indicates the baskets.

Clola is trying to get away from Kemnay's hands so she can investigate the basket. Though she has just had breakfast, she is always willing to have another meal. He holds her up, looks into her eyes and says firmly, "No, that is lunch. You will wait." She makes as if to bite him, but decides that there is much to do this day, so instead settles on his shoulder and goes to sleep.

Kemnay tells Balgavney of his time in his village, about the loss of his parents, his encounter with the Mad Trader and the mystery of Achath's disappearance. It takes all morning.

She listens carefully and then asks him, "You think the one you call the Mad Trader is Garmond? That they are the same person and somehow he has managed to steal your friend?" The look on her face is skeptical.

"I am sure they are the same person," Paddler says. "When you talked of him, I heard her voice in my heart saying to remember and his name. I don't know how he managed to overpower her, but somehow he did. I think she is trapped here somewhere. At least I hope she is -- I fear she may be lost still." He looks across the valley towards the statue. He is sure that somehow it is involved. Under his breath he says, "I won't give up, Achath, I promise."

"I am not sure how knowing this will help us," Balgavney says evenly. "I don't know that what he did was right, but he has done no real evil here. Fintray's panic is what caused the souls to be trapped. He would have brought notice on himself if he had been involved in the loss of a wise woman. Surely he could not have escaped the gods notice if he had truly harmed a wise one. We are well protected."

"I know that you are, which is what make it all the more curious," the man says with some confusion. "Unless I have only just imagined her voice out of hope for finding her."

Balgavney says earnestly, "Never give up hope. It is the second most important thing in our life after love. I think if your friend lives, she will wait for you, and even if she does not, wouldn't you still want to find her soul and set it to rest?" The kindness in her eyes is deep and Kemnay is comforted by it. In this moment the weight of her years is not so sad a thing.

The man reaches for the lunch basket, which wakes the dragon. He sets food out for her and quickly eats some himself. Balgavney joins them and they have a thoughtful meal.

After they have finished, she says, "I think now you must find Fintray and Garmond to talk with them. I know they are in the valley with you, in some form, but I am unsure of where. We must find them and see if there is a way to bring the last-life souls back, so that we can break this endless cycle. Perhaps this will help us find your friend and find a way to free your parents as well. I can see that it makes you sad to know they are trapped."

"Yes, it would be good if my search could be at an end, but your need is much greater," the man says compassionately. "I need to know what happened to drive you out of the valley, why the children can come and go freely across the barrier and who else can cross it. I will need to know that I can talk to the last-life souls here."

Balgavney smiles "You have many questions, I will answer as best I can. There was a great panic in the village the night of the disaster. As I told you I had been sitting with my daughter, Skirza and saw her turn to stone, but my grief was cut short because soon I had many frightened people pounding on my door. I put her stone on the hearth so it would be safe and went to talk to the people of the village.

"At my door was everyone in the village who was still living, all telling me the same story. They heard a terrible voice and suddenly someone they loved turned to stone. I looked up the hill towards Rora Moss' home and saw a great light flowing around it. I was sure Fintray and Garmond were the cause of the situation and as soon as I could calm the villagers down I was going to go up there and force them to fix what they had done.

"I managed to calm people and told them each to go back to their home and carefully set the stones together on the hearth so they would be safe, then to meet me at the village circle. I made my way carefully up the hill, feeling a great and terrible magic building. At the top of the hill I found the melded Wolf Angel and demanded it tell me what had happened. I tried to get them to unmeld so that I could talk with Fintray, but the fear that had driven her to do this in the first place was still strong around her. Garmond was helpless to break away from her.

"'Fintray,' I shouted over the rising wind, 'you must come out and talk with me. You must undo this before dawn.'

"The great voice of the Wolf Angel rolled over me. 'I will not,' it cried. 'I will never let it be undone.' The fear-driven child was still in control, and he terrible voice continued: 'Know that at dawn you will all leave this place. Only a few may return, and never to the village. I will keep you protected, I will keep you fed, but you will not take my mother away from me, ever.'

"Then suddenly the wind blew hard enough to knock me from my feet. When I managed to right myself they were gone and I have never seen them again. I tried to go into Rora Moss' home, but could not cross the gateway. I returned to the village circle and found many frightened and unhappy faces awaiting me. They had heard the Wolf Angel's voice and knew that there was no choice.

"I told them to go back to their homes and bring the stones back to this circle, hoping I could help save something in the situation by putting all the stones within its magical protection. I went to my own home, but when I tried again to touch the stone that was my daughter, my hand could not reach it. I went to every house, every place in the village. All of the stones were safe, but we could not touch or move them. I knew my chance had been lost in the first moments, before I understood what had happened and why. All I could do was to help my people gather what they could of their lives and flee.

"We took what we could carry from the village, and at dawn a great wind pushed us away and we could never return. We went over the hill and sent word to a nearby isle, then started the building of our new village that very day. There we have been ever since. As to who can cross the barrier, any that farm the land can come to work the fields and they can still ask for the rain as they need. Tifty was heavy with the twins when she crossed over, which is why they can come and go across the barrier, at least until they become adults. Any child that was unborn at the crossing can come and go, even into Rora Moss' home, but they cannot move the stones. We have tried to get them to, but they all say the same thing, that if they try to touch the stones, the Wolf Angel shouts at them. So they leave flowers for her at the statue, so she will be happy and let them play in the garden."

Kemnay nods. He now understands much more. He asks, "Did not another bonded pair try to cross?"

"Oh yes," Balgavney replies. "Pitsligo and Duffus tried several times to cross. They could go into the fields and even nearly to the statue at the bottom, but could not get to the house or into the village. They did manage to free the fishing boats so that they drifted out of the bay and the fisher-folk recovered many of them, but that was all that could be done. You are the first person to be in the village for a very long time. This gives us hope."

"I am glad it gives you hope," the man says, "but I don't know what I can do. I am able to touch the stones, but I can't see how that helps." He looks earnestly at the wise woman. "I would be glad of any suggestions you might give me."

"I have spent much time talking with the elders and we have decided if you can move the stones to the circle in the village, perhaps that would help bring Fintray and Garmond out of hiding. We think you should not, however, try to move or even touch Rora Moss, Strathy or Cullerlie. For now, let them rest. Of all the stones, those will be the most watched." Balgavney's voice shook with feeling.

Kemnay nods. He also believes this is the best way to start. "Clola and I will do this tomorrow, if for no other reason that to get them into our protection. I will speak to any I can, if you want." He looks at the wise woman, wondering if she would ask him to speak to her daughter.

"It would be better not to wake them -- it might alert Fintray to what we are doing," the wise woman says with a tear on her face. "As much as I would send and have word from my daughter, I do not want her to know that she is trapped."

"I will not wake them," Kemnay promises, once again frustrated that he cannot go to this woman and offer comfort. "I will only move them carefully."

"For now that will be enough. Perhaps we can return them to life and let them live it out as normally as they can, but in the meantime it is best to let them be unaware." The wise woman's face was sad.

"I am going to go out into the bay in my boat for a while this afternoon," Kemnay tells her loudly. "It helps me to think. Tonight I will let Clola catch us some food, so tell Tifty not to worry about feeding us supper this day. Also, can you ask the village children who can cross the barrier to come the tomorrow with you." His voice drops to a quieter tone. "If I succeed in moving the stones, I want to have some distraction. Tell them to play noisy games, tell stories and laugh as much as they can. Stay close and encourage them. I think perhaps the sound of happy laughter might take attention away from what I plan to do."

It is a thin plan, but the best he can come up with on short notice. The wise woman nods in agreement and stands. "Thank you, Kemnay, it would please me greatly to know my daughter is truly safe." She turns and walks away quietly.

The man sits watching her and then turns to look down at the statue. He grabs Clola off his shoulder and tosses her into the air suddenly. She is startled and shifts to a larger form to chase him down the hill, but he makes it to the cover of the trees before she can catch him. At camp he grabs his boat and dumps the remaining gear out of it, then takes his paddle up and gets to the water just as he hears the dragon coming through the trees behind him. He gets into the boat and paddles strongly out into the water. He knows she will do her best to dump him in the water and he wants to be as ready as he can be to prevent it or dunk her as well.

When she comes out of the trees and sees him in the boat, she shifts to her blue sea form and goes under the waves. This gives her a slight advantage over flying as she has no wings for him to catch. but he also can hit her on a sensitive spot with the paddle. After an hour or so of being dumped out of his boat, Kemnay calls a truce and asks her to fish for them. She is willing and comes back with many crabs. They have a tasty supper and talk quietly about what they will do in the morning.

Kemnay sits by the fireside talking with Clola, who is bloated with crabs. She has had especially good luck fishing this day and they are both well fed.

"Little One," he says casually, unsure of who might be listening despite the ward around the glade, "tomorrow I think I will go explore the village and see if there is a house that we might mend to stay in. We will be here for the season of storms now and camping is fine for short periods, but if we can live within walls all the better." For now he wants to keep his actual intent quiet. Though he and Balgavney had discussed it, there is so much other discussion and history he feels this would distract from what he hoped to achieve.

The dragon looks up at him, catching his unsaid message and yawns. " I suppose it is a good idea, but you will have to look at all of them carefully. It will have to be the best of a bad lot, I'm afraid."

The man replies casually, "I expect you are right. I will search the gardens as well for more food for us. I like crabs, but even they will get old after a while." He is casually drawing on the ground with a stick that has been burned in the fire, quietly building a spell of distraction. He is not sure if they can act directly against Fintray and Garmond, especially since they haven't located them yet, but he is fairly sure he can move the last-life stones in the village and the protection of the stone circle if he has enough time and doesn't hesitate.

The dragon looks bored and draws into his pattern with her claw, adding to the protection. "Well, make sure you take along a bag and the basket. There might be pumpkins, after all." The dragon burps cheerfully. "I think I will nap in the sun tomorrow. I worked hard with the fishing today." She yawns hugely.

"For tonight, I am tired and just want to sleep." The man walks over to his fire as he speaks, then flops on the bed roll. The dragon joins him.

In silent talk, she says to him, "I will play with the children tomorrow. You will have to hurry and not hesitate. If you are caught in your grief we may fail. Be careful when you handle those stones."

"I know," Paddler replies, just as silently. "I am warned now and ready for it, and I don't want to risk waking the souls trapped in them. This is too important to chance. Trust me, Clola, I will not fail Balgavney." He yawns and drifts off to sleep watching the fire.

Moving stones

In the morning he walks up the hill to meet Balgavney. She has about a dozen children under the age of ten storm seasons with her, as well as Ythsie and Skene. They have a basket from Tifty with some sweet breads and cream for him and some pumpkin cake for the dragon.

At the bottom of the basket, under some straw, is a leather bag sewn with magical designs on it. Kemnay looks at it and glances at Balgavney who catches his eye and nods, just for an instant. This is where the stones must be carried.

The children and the dragon start a very noisy game of tag in the upper field and Kemnay says loudly to Balgavney, "I am going down to the village to see if there is a house we might mend to stay in for the winter. Do you think Tifty might allow me to borrow this basket, so that if I find food in the gardens I could carry it back?" His eyes seriously watch the red-haired wise woman, but his face is a smiling mask.

Balgavney is laughing and watching the children, who have figured out that the dragon cannot cross the barrier so it is easy to duck out of her reach, even if she shifts. It is a loud and merry game.

The wise woman says casually, "That is a good idea. I am sure there are pumpkins gone wild there. I know how fond Clola is of them. Go ahead and use the basket, and you can bring it back up later. I know Tifty has put some lunch for you in it as well. I am going to sit here in the sun with the children and knit." She sits down on a blanket and pulls needles and wool from her basket and her hands start to fly.

"Thank you, Balgavney," he says with a light voice. "I expect Clola would be happier playing with the children here, so I'll search without her. Oh, I need to take my water bag back to camp. I'll go that way." He waves to the wise woman and heads down the river path to his camp. He wants to stay away from the statue for now.

Once inside his ward, he brings out the magical bag and looks at it. He arranges it in the bottom of the basket so that it is open at the top and spread out on the bottom. Even if he puts other things in the basket, he will still be able to slip the stones in.

He takes the other path to the village, quietly reaching out with his senses and does not find himself at all closely watched. Between the wards and the distraction of the children, he has a very good chance of success.

Once at the village he knows he must search very quickly, but carefully as well. From Balgavney's story, he knows that most all of the stones were put on hearths, but what of people that had no one with them when it happened? They might be lost in the dust of their home, and he must recover them all.

He walks into the first building, which is the pub. On the hearth are three stones, but for a moment he ignores them and makes a show of looking around the building and checking the woodwork. He sets the basket down by the hearth and looks up the chimney. Poking at a bird's nest, he creates a small cloud of dust and sneezes, then sits for a moment and looks around the room.

"Well, this place will not do." He stands and bends over for the basket. For a moment he holds his breath, then quickly takes up the stones and drops them into the bag inside the basket. He walks out of the pub and goes to the next building.

By midmorning he has searched every building in the village and has twenty-three stones. He walks around the outside of the village, casually searching kitchen gardens. He has found some pumpkins and gathered a couple of small ones, as well as some herbs. He has walked around casually talking to himself about the condition of the buildings, the things he found in the gardens and the number of bird's nests in all the chimneys.

Wandering up the hill, he approaches the village magic circle. The flowers are bright within it and he is within a few steps of the opening. As he approaches it, he feels some tension in the magic around him. Something has turned its attentions to him. He sits down within sight of the circle, but with his back intentionally to it and makes a production out of pulling lunch out of the basket.

As he relaxes with his meal, Clola lands beside him with a thump. She immediately puts her nose in the basket and pulls the cord on the magic bag closed, then demands a portion of his lunch. He shares lunch with her and asks about the game. She complains that the children cheat by hiding in beyond her reach.

"Well, Little One," he says lightly, "they need some advantage. After all, none of them can fly." He laughs at the dragon, who once again puts her head in the basket.

In silent talk, he tells her, "When I go close to the stone circle the watching increases. I do not think they will let me just walk across and I am sure I will need you as well. We need an idea." His brow furrows as he thinks about it.

"Trust me," Clola says with a hint of mischief. "I have an idea."

"That is usually my first mistake," he replies, and starts packing lunch away.

Clola jumps into the basket. "You found pumpkins," she says with delight, shifting slightly larger. "I love pumpkins." She is rocking the basket as if to tip it over. She puts her head into it and gets hold of the top of the magic bag. As the basket rocks, Kemnay leaps towards it.

"Stop that! You are going to spill it and I'll be chasing pumpkins down the hill," he shouts at her. He grabs the basket edge and rocks it towards him. She shifts slightly larger and sends the basket toppling over at him, then lands on his tunic and quickly stuffs the magic bag into the neck of it.

He feels the bag, realises what she has done, and understands what she has in mind. He grabs her and they start to wrestle. She shifts until she is about the same size. The fight moves around the field closer to the opening, and when he is standing in front of it, she suddenly shifts large and leaps on him, overbalancing him through the gateway.

He lands flat on his back with her sitting on him, inside the circle. They have succeeded in getting themselves and the stones into the circle. Kemnay whispers his thanks to her, but scolds her for all the new bruises.

"We are here," she said smugly. "That is all that matters." She looks out of the circle and sees dust building into a windstorm and says urgently, "Hurry, Kemnay, they are coming."

Kemnay takes the bag out of his shirt. Kneeling in the centre of the circle, he shouts to the gods, "Bless these souls and keep them safe." He sets the bag on the ground and scrapes a bit of dirt over it. This is enough to make the blessing stick and he knows he has done what is needed. Now the question is if he is going to be able to leave this place.

At the entrance of the circle stands the beautiful and terrible form of the Wolf Angel.

Wolf Angel appears

For a moment Kemnay looks in wonder at the strange form. How different, yet the same it is as the statues he has found. He stands up purposefully and dusts off his hands, then lifts Clola, who has returned to her normal size, to his shoulder. He walks over to the gateway and stops.

"Fintray and Garmond, I have need to speak with you," the man says quietly. "There is much healing needed in this place and it will be easier with your help." He stands, waiting to see what will happen.

For a moment, he is convinced that the Wolf Angel will flee and he will have to go searching for them. Slowly, however, the form dissolves before his eyes, becoming two separate beings: an angry young woman with angel wings, and a black wolf at her feet.

"How dare you steal the people of my village!" the angel woman shouts at him. There are tears on her face as she pauses and looks down at the wolf. "Thank you. We have been trapped together for a long time. Long enough for me to realise the damage I had done, yet not long enough to learn how to change it." Her face was very sad.

Encouraged by her mixed reaction, Kemnay sits on the ground just inside the gateway. He is not yet ready to step out of the circle's protection. Clola slides down from his shoulder to his lap, so that she can also watch the strange pair before her.

Fintray spreads her great wings and settles to the grass outside of the gate, for the moment accepting that the separation is not a bad thing for either side. Garmond lays down by her knees with his great head resting on his paws.

Kemnay says quietly, "It is not finished yet. There is more to do and some of it you will have to do yourself."

He watches the pair closely for signs of sudden change of emotion. He does not totally trust them, after hearing Balgavney's story.

Fintray looks steadily at him and then drops her eyes. "I know what you say is true, but I don't know if I can do it." Her voice is like a whisper in the wind.

"You must," Kemnay says matter-of-factly. "There is no one else who can."

"But I don't want to lose my mother." Fintray starts to cry, putting her head in her hands. Garmond moves slightly away from her, as if afraid she may grab him again, then relents and pushes his nose against her face. She lets her hands drop and pets the wolf reassuringly.

"'How long have you been without her? How very many years?" Kemnay says roughly. "You have survived all this time with just Garmond." Kemnay's voice softens. " I understand losing your parents. I lost my own the same way you did. It is hard and terrible, but I still do what I must. You have a task in this place and you are failing in it." His face was stern.

His harsh words made Fintray flinch. All bonded pairs have a strong sense of responsibility to their task and their people. To be accused by another pair of failing was a deep blow indeed.

The young woman leans forward, outrage showing in her face. "I am not failing," she screams at the man sitting before her. "I am still protecting them. They aren't hurt." She points behind him.

He remains calm, but grateful he had stayed inside the village circle. He does not want to fight with the pair, but work with them to save the people.

He says as soothingly as he can, "No, these souls are not hurt, though they are numb and in darkness, with no hope. What about the people of the village you chased from their homes and have trapped into the same incarnation over and over? What of Balgavney, who has for eight hundred storm seasons tried to reach you and help? What of Tifty and her children? How can you say you have done no hurt or are not failing? The truth of it is that you have done great hurt here and it is time to repair it."

Fintray's face shows deep shock. "Eight hundred storm seasons?" she says in horror. "No, it can't be that long. You are lying to me." She is shaking her head violently, trying to deny the truth she is hearing. "Balgavney is still here? No one is here but us and the last-life souls. The rest went over the hill and went on without us."

Clola speaks up, "Yes, they went over the hill and made a new village, but they could not go on. They were cast outside the wheel of birth and rebirth. There must be a balance of souls in a village or town for it to survive. If there are too many of one kind of soul, the gods send others. If there are too few, the town dies and nothing is left. Because you took all of these people out of the cycle, the people they were connected to by love or family are trapped here. Until the balance is restored, they will never be free to go on. They can only relive the same life, over and over, always grieving for the lost and praying to the gods for a change. Just because you destroyed this village by driving people away, does not mean you did not hurt them greatly." The dragon snorts in disdain. "If you don't believe me, walk up to the top of the hill and ask Balgavney yourself. She is there waiting, as she has been all of her many lives."

Fintray looks up the hill. She can see the children playing in the sun and it looks, for a moment, as if she might go up. Instead she looks down at Garmond and asks, "Is this true, what they are saying? Have I done this terrible thing?"

Garmond looks at her sadly and replies, "Yes, Wingling. This pair speak only the truth to you. We have done terrible things, you and I. I believe now that the time has come where we must pay for it and accept what the gods will do to us."

The wolf looks at the man and says, "There is more, is there not?"

Kemnay nods. "Now have I learned your other name. I always called you Trader or Mad Trader. Did you take the wise woman Achath?" He has a small hope in his heart, but Kemnay is sure if she had heard that he was near, she would let him know. He fears where she might be or that she may be lost forever.

Garmond nods sadly. "I tricked her and trapped her."

Achath's story

When Paddler and Achath kissed, the Mad Trader had been watching in the shadow of the trees. It was the first time he had seen the man and the young woman together and now he knew how he could force the one with strong magic to help him. He also knew how he could get the gods to let him alone. He felt their gaze on him all the time and hid as well as he could, but unless he could get a companion to protect him, he had no hope of being able to escape their notice forever. He slipped into the darkness and waited by the path for the woman to come.

Just before dawn the oldster breathed his last and Achath whispered prayers over him, rejoicing in his life. She did what she could to settle the family and walked out into the weak light of morning to go back to Merry. She was thinking of the kiss she had stolen from Paddler and was distracted as she walked up the path.

At a dark corner near the dock a form stepped out in front of her. For a moment she was startled, but then realised it was only the trader who was a friend to Merry. Achath was uneasy with the man, but she understood his troubled heart.

"Please Achath, can you help me?" His voice seemed pained. He was holding his left arm close to his body, and it seemed to be bleeding. "I fell getting onto my boat and have cut myself. I know you are a healer -- can you look at it?" He was standing in the tree shadow and the light was very dim.

Compassionately, she walked over to him, trying to see. "Of course I will help you, Trader, but we need to get to more light. Let us go to Merry's home and she can help as well." The young healer spoke soothingly to him. Her scarf caught on a near branch and pulled off, but before she could turn back for it the man seemed to wobble a bit and she got distracted and forgot about it. She could get it in a moment or two.

Trader knew he had only a short time to get the woman to come with him and make his escape. If he could get her on his boat, then he could be gone before that dragon would be able to catch him. His plan required him only to get away safely and the dragon was his only risk. He must convince this woman to come of her own will.

He took a step towards her and deliberately staggers. "I feel a little light headed and dizzy," he said with a weak voice. Achath quickly went over to him and put an arm around his shoulder to steady him. "My boat is nearer, can we go there? I have a good lamp and healing herbs," he said, again seeming to stumble.

Achath was afraid he would faint and agreed to go with him. When they got to the boat, the man seemed to get a little stronger, but there was blood seeping through the cloth on his arm and she was worried. She helped him up the ladder and then followed him. He went ahead and suddenly there was a strong light, she felt a slight lurching of the boat, but was distracted by the man talking to her.

"Thank you so much, dear lady, for being willing to help me," Trader said, stumbling around the cabin of the boat, causing it to rock slightly. In his seemingly absent movements to the cabin he had managed to throw off the rope that held him to the dock. He knew the outgoing tide would carry him away from the village. He had also managed to close the magical ward around the boat so it couldn't be seen. He had done this while distracting the young wise woman, so that she had relaxed her own personal ward and come into his created circle of power.

Finally, after a look out the window confirmed they were indeed in motion, he seemed to collapse into a heap on the floor. Achath knelt down and pulled his arm gently away from his body. His face had pain on it and she smoothed his brow as she would any injured person. She was concerned when she looked at his wound. His forearm was slashed, the cut was deep, but clean. She put medicines on it and gently stitched the wound closed. He flinched and moaned a bit, but didn't seem to wake, which she was glad of. She tried not to hurt anyone, but sometimes healing caused hurt; it couldn't be helped. Just as she finished sewing the wound and dressing it, he seemed to wake and look at her with calculating eyes. He struggled to sit up, then kneel so he was looking down at her.

"Thank you, Achath," the mad man said darkly. "You have done more than you will ever know."

She looked startled and in that moment of inattention, he lifted his right fist and hit her suddenly on the jaw so that she fell unconscious on the deck. She didn't have time to send for help, as she was totally taken by surprise. He knew he was still close enough to the village that she might try to swim or call out for help. He had to keep her quiet until they were well away. He locked the woman in the back cabin, making sure she had food and water, and went up on deck and rigged his sails. The winds were with him and he made very fast time away.

Achath woke in darkened room with a very small, round window letting in some weak daylight. For a moment she was confused by the motion she was feeling, and then the memory of what had happened jarred her upright. Trader had tricked her onto his boat and somehow left the village. She reached out for her ward, but found her protections had been stripped from her. For the first time she began to be afraid.

There was food and water on a nearby table, so she took a moment to feed herself and look around the room that had become her prison. The wooden walls were traced with a web of silver metal, and all of the patterns led to a small shelf which held a plain grey stone. She could not get close enough to the shelf to touch the stone, but suspected that it was what was holding her helpless. She tried the door, but soon found it to be locked. When she looked out of the window, all she could see was water, stretching forever. She settled herself to wait until her captor decided to show himself to her.

A short time later the door opened and there sat Trader on the floor outside of the room. She could not cross the threshold, but she sat upon the floor so she might look into his eyes and know if he lied to her.

Once she had settled, the dark man spoke quietly to her. "First, let me say to you, Achath, that I am sorry. I did not want to hurt you, but I had to have you come with me to a place where you had no choice but to listen to me."

The woman looked at him levelly. "Could you not have just asked me for a private talk in the village, Trader? You know that all wise ones are bound to help when they can," the young woman said in a slightly reproving tone.

"Yes," he said, looking a bit guilty, "I might have asked, but I believed you would not consider my request without this." He pointed to the room around her. "As you see, I have a wish stone from the gods. It holds you there, but cannot bend you to my will. I must on my own convince you to aid me."

Achath felt a slight dread in her heart. A gods' wish stone was a very powerful thing indeed.

She asked, "How is it that you come to have such a powerful thing? It is not usually something a mortal can hold."

He replied, with a crafty look, "Actually I stole it from the house of my father. I am only half mortal, so I can possess it without much harm, though sometimes it speaks to me in many voices and drives my mind into restlessness."

Achath nodded. That would explain his sudden and difficult shifts of mood -- to hold such a stone cost dearly. She asked again, "Why am I here? I cannot touch or wield such a stone. As wise as I am, this is beyond me. Do you think to use me as a blood price?"

This brought a look of shock to the man's dark face. "No!" he shouted, "I would not pay a blood price, even if I were lost. I am not evil. I swear to you, I am only afraid." He calmed down. "Know, dear lady, that I would free you, even at my own cost, before I would spill your blood. That sin would take me beyond all hope. You are my hope and my last one. I have searched long, hiding from the gods, for the right person to help me."

Achath believed him to be sincere, though his words were confusing to her. In her calmest voice, she told him, "Trader, I would listen to you, even without the force of the stone holding me here. Tell me what it is you need and I will consider it for its own merit. I will not hold it against you that you have tricked me, but I would ask you to take me back to my village once I have heard you. I am much-needed there."

"I cannot do that," he said flatly. "You will stay there until you agree to do what I need or be exiled with me if the gods find me first. You are the last hope I have." His voice was sad. "I am sorry, but no matter what happens, you will never return there."

This caused Achath to stand up and turn her back on him. Tears fell down her face as she looked out the window. To never see Merry again or Paddler, to never laugh at the mischief of Little One or help birth another baby! Was this man such a monster as to put his own needs above that of an entire village? Turning slightly, she looked at the wish stone and decided that he was, to have stolen something so terrible. It was obvious that stealing her life would be nothing too drastic, despite his protests about not spilling her blood.

She heard the door close behind her and supposed he had gone. From the way he stayed beyond the door, it showed her that he feared her magic. If she could get through his ward, perhaps she could do something to get the gods' attention drawn to him. It was a sure thing they would be looking for him. Only the twisted power of the wish stone kept him from their sight. How long he could hold that was a guess she couldn't make.

Exhausted from her strong emotion and still feeling a bit of a headache from his blow to her jaw, she fell back into the bed and slept. In her dreams, she saw Paddler in his boat, searching, and she hoped it was for her. She tried to call out to him, but her voice was lost in the winds. In her sleep she cried and woke to wetness on her pillow. In the morning she found fresh water and food on the table and a basin with washing water and drying clothes, as well as a change of clothing. She recognised it as her own and suspected that he had stolen it from Merry's house the night he took her.

The young woman ate and washed, dressed in clean clothing, then took time to scrub the clothing she had been wearing and neaten up the cabin around her. All she could do was wait for him to return and the time passed slowly. She wondered if he would wear her down with boredom since she was used to being active and around other people. She was feeling very lonely and not a little frightened. What was going to happen to her? What did this mad man want that would cost her everything, and yet leave her alive? So many questions and the answers beyond her reach.

Near sunset on the second day, she once again heard footsteps outside the door and, as expected, the door opened. She went and sat down just inside, facing her captor. She said to him, "If it is your intent to leave me here until I become as mad as you are with boredom, it won't help me to listen to you." Her voice was sharp, though she tried to calm her growing anger.

He looked startled. "It was not my intent that you be bored. I hadn't thought about it. I have no books and I cannot allow you to wander around the boat until you agree to do what I want. I have only cloth and threads in my cargo." His voice was distracted. He needed her cooperation and was not prepared for her anger.

"That will do," Achath said. "I would be happy for cloth and sewing threads. I assume you did not take much of my clothing from Merry's house?" Her brow arched in question.

He looked sheepishly at her and replied, "Only what I could quickly grab and hide in my shirt. I did not know how long it would take me to convince you, but I thought having some of your own clothing would help make you comfortable."

Achath said honestly to him, "I thank you for that kindness, but I must needs keep my hands busy as well. If you will give me sewing to do, that would help."

She decided that whatever his failings, he did have some caring in him. She also decided that she needed to hear what he wanted in full so she could think about in and come to terms with what she would be able to do. There had to be some hope. As a wise woman, he could trick her for a short time, but only a very short time. She was strong in her own right.

"All right, Trader," she said firmly. "Today you will tell me what it is that you want from me, so that I may think about it." She stood up and took a blanket and pillow from the bed and made a comfortable place on the floor to sit, so that he would realise she was ready to listen to him.

He nodded to her, then took a flask of wine and poured some into two mugs. Hers he pushed through the doorway with a broom handle until it was just across the threshold. He was careful not to get so close to the door that he might fall through or be knocked off balance. The ward only kept her in. If he fell within her reach, what little power he had over her would be lost and she would break out and be able to call the gods to her aid. He couldn't risk that.

Achath noted his cautions and came to the same conclusions. His power over her was very limited, which gave her some hope of escape.

She looked at him and told him with her eyes that she was willing to test his limits.

She took up the mug of wine and had a small taste of it. He did the same and then began to talk.

"As I said, I am half mortal. My mother is human and my father one of the gods, though she would never say exactly which one. I often thought she lied to me, until I realised that I can hear the gods when they talk and not many others can. Sometimes their voices get so loud in my head." He sipped the wine cautiously.

"I have wandered the seas all of my life, first with my mother to escape the cruelty of villagers that didn't understand why I was different. Later, I did it out of habit. My mother found a place to settle and her life was content, especially once I had left. I visit her village from time to time and since I am full grown now, not many know who I am." There was sadness in his eyes and Achath felt compassion for this damaged soul. His life was not easy.

"In my wandering I came across a lone man living on a remote isle. His village had been destroyed by raiders and he was the sole survivor. He said he was a wise one, left with a message and a warning for me. He was very old when I found him and near to death. He told me that the reason for my birth was to bind a soul to the outside of the wheel, so that no matter how long folks lived the cycle of birth and rebirth, they would never all go to the quiet lands. As long as one remained, the gods would have power over all, except the last-life, the wise, and the bonded, who they could touch only lightly. I was to be the soul chained in the darkness for all time."

Achath looked at him in horror. Such a fate was often told of in scary stories by the fireside, but to meet a soul in such jeopardy was more terrible than the worst of tales. As unhappy as she was to be his captive, she was beginning to understand the desperation that moved him.

The choice is made

Trader drank more of the wine and rushed on to tell her the rest. The pity in her eyes hurt him and wounded the child in his heart. He couldn't be angry at her because she was an honest, caring woman. His hope was small, but still there.

The mad man continued, "You can imagine I was not happy to learn this and I took to spying on the gods. I don't believe they realised that I knew the fate they intended for me. The old one died just after I arrived, so it is possible I could have missed his message. The gods laughed among themselves, though I found out that not all of them shared the plan. I went back to the world to wander, not knowing what else I could do. I didn't know how long it would before they would take me, but I knew that they did not move quickly. Their lives are measured differently than mortal ones, so there was no hurry for them, while I was desperate for safety."

Achath nodded. She could read the truth on him and knew that he was not lying to her. He was desperate or he would not be doing all that he had done, but she was still uneasy with her place in his plans.

He went on, "As I wandered, I talked to as many wise ones as I could find and some last-life souls as well. I wanted to find out if there was a way to save myself. One night I stumbled into a village on an isle so remote and more seasons away than I care to remember. There was much surprise when my boat came up to the dock. In the village, I found an unusual bonded pair. The companion, Murkie, was a hunting tiger, beautiful and terrible. The human, Creag, was a musician of no special skill, unless his companion was touching him. Together they kept the place hidden from the gods' eyes. Their village was happy and all were well fed. The normal cycle of life continued, and it seemed like a small slice of paradise to my eyes."

"One night by the fireside I was talking to Creag about my worry. He was the first bonded one I had been able to talk to, as the noise from a bonded pair usually made my brain hurt and I often was considered mad because of it. This night, Murkie came and laid her great head on my lap and the noise all stopped. It was the first time I could remember in my long life that my thoughts were just my own. I looked at her in wonder."

"Murkie asked me, 'You are god touched?' I nodded silently, so she looked at me more deeply and said, 'Ah, I see. You are a god-child like me.' I was sent reeling by what she said and begged her to explain what she meant. She looked at Creag and he nodded and began to play his small harp softly. Suddenly it was just Murkie and I in a quiet pocket of protected darkness. I realised his magic had made a safe place for us to talk, but left the illusion of us still sitting listening to his music to keep others unaware of our conversation." Trader took more wine and continued his tale.

"Murkie told me that she too had been a god-child, that I was not the first half mortal. She was to be a breeder for a new race of mixed bloods. She had been my intended mate, until she took herself off the wheel by becoming a companion. That was the time it was decided to chain me in darkness. I begged her to tell me how she had done this."

"She said she found out what was happening and fled into the wild lands. She found a wise one, left wounded by raiders, and healed him. He told her how to rescue herself and gave her a wish stone he had hidden that had protected him. He told her she must bear a child and trade its new soul for her own to become a companion. It was best to have a wise one to help with the trade, but it would require trickery. She took his advice and went looking for a small village. She arrived here and made friends with the wise one and he took her to wife, never realising what she was. The wish stone hid her. When she was with child, she confessed to her husband and begged his help. He loved the woman well and decided to help her."

"When the child was born, they invoked the wish stone. Murkie became the tiger and bonded to the wise soul that had moved to the child. The new soul was a last-life and locked into the wish stone. The tiger told the story in the village that the woman had died giving birth to the child and the she as guardian had arrived to watch over him. The wise man was said to have fallen over a cliff a short time after the birth, leaving the orphan child with his companion to be cared for by all the village. So the tiger had escaped the gods and kept her love. As a pair bonded by love, they were greatly able to protect and care for their village and stay out of sight of the gods."

"Her story gave me hope," the Mad Trader said as he drank from his cup again, "but I need a woman to help me, as I can not bear my own child. I have two choices to survive," he said sadly, "Either I must find a wise woman to bear a child, willing to make the same trade and be bonded with me or I must bind a wise soul to the wish stone to force the trade with a willing woman bearing my child and put that wise one back to being a last-life soul. That soul could not go back on the wise path, though -- it would be forced into the quiet lands forever." He had the good grace to look unhappy, while still being resolute.

Achath sat quietly, thinking about what he had told her. Her choice to become a wise woman was a serious one, and his story worried her.

The young woman said softly, "These are not choices I am willing to make. I will think about what you have said. I ask you now to provide me with food, with sewing and to leave me for a few days to see if there is another way. You must understand I am not, at this moment, willing to be bonded to you and I have chosen the wise way and wish to remain there. I do not want to be banished to the quiet lands, because my work is here." Her voice was firm.

He nodded and got up from the floor. He returned a short time later with a plate of food, a jar of water and a bundle of cloth. These he carefully pushed through the doorway with the stick. Achath accepted his offerings and asked him to close the door and leave her for a day to think. She took up the cloth and began sewing, her mind a whirl at what she had learned.

Trader returned in a day and asked her if she was ready to make a choice. She told him she was not. He told her that they would be making port soon, but she would not be able to escape. The wish stone held her in the small room and even if the boat sank on the rocks, she would be trapped within its sphere. Every day he returned to her to ask, and every day she would not answer or agree. She only told him over and over her path was the wise one, and she would not want leave it.
Trader believed she would not bear him a child, so he was sure that all he could do was bind her. He had to find a woman who would do this for him. In the village he had stopped in, he found the woman Rora Moss. When he was sure she was with child, he returned to his boat and left the bay.

This area was heavy with people and sea traffic, and he needed a quiet place to work. He found a sheltered cove with a stone arch that held a good place to tie a boat. He set the boat in such a way that the next storms would tear it away from its ropes and dash it to pieces on the rocks. There would be no traces left of him or the young wise woman; the sea would have it all. Then he worked the first part of his terrible magic.

For the last time he went to the door of the cabin where the wise woman Achath was held. The wish stone had kept her safe. She could not harm herself, even if she would violate her vows as a wise one and try. She knew that the end had been reached. The look in his eyes told her this. She sat on the floor to talk with him, for what would be the last time, hoping desperately that she could convince him to free her and give up his mad plan.

Trader sat on the floor and asked her, "Have you chosen? Will you bear me a child and bond with me?"

"I will not," she said firmly. "I am a wise woman, and I would not change that, even to save you."

"Then you leave me no choice. I have found a woman and she carries my child. Tonight I bind your soul to the wish stone." He looked at her seriously. "Know that I am sorry for this, and if there was another way, I would take it, but there is not." He stood up and walked towards the doorway for the first time in her sight. She found she was too overwhelmed by what she had heard to move. He threw a spell at her that held her in place.

Trader's face was a terrible blackness as he crossed the barrier, he shouted, "I, Garmond, half child of the gods invoke the wish stone to do my will and bind this woman Achath to my purpose."

Once the stone was invoked, Garmond changed into a great wolf, his human memories weakened. He took the wish stone up in his mouth and leaped off the boat. He set the stone down for a moment and chewed at the moorings, knowing that this would help the boat go adrift when the storms came. He went to the village and buried the stone in the fields behind it, marking the place so that later he could protect it, and went to the wise woman Balgavney to carry out his terrible trade.

Achath had stood, prepared to fight, but also prepared to do something desperate if she had to. She knew she would have only a moment, perhaps only a heart beat to act. Now, held helpless in place, her chances were even slimmer.

As Garmond spoke the words, she felt the magic building around her. With the last of her will, she whispered urgently, "Kemnay, remember: Garmond." Then she was gone.

Paddler spent many seasons searching for Achath, sure that he would find some trace of her or the mad trader. He never knew what had happened to them, never knew the choice she had been forced into. It seemed as though they had dropped from the earth, but still he kept searching.

Reconciliations

After the wolf tells Achath's story to them, this time it is Kemnay whose grief brings tears on his face. Fintray looks at her companion, astonished that he would or could do such to a wise woman. The lengths he has gone to protect himself are great. She loves her companion, even after learning his deeds, and wants to save him from the darkness. Her resolve begins to go towards doing what is needed.

Kemnay does his best to stop his tears, as there is still much work to do here. "So where is she now? Has she become Rora Moss? Is she trapped in that house up the hill?" Kemnay pleads with the wolf.

Garmond shakes his great head, and says uncertainly, "I am not sure, I think she is trapped in a stone. We would need to read all of the stones and this is beyond our skills."

Kemnay says sharply, "It is not beyond mine. This I have done all my life." He looks at Fintray and ask her pointedly, "Are you ready now? There are many here besides me who are hurt. Will you help me restore them?"

Fintray stands and shifts back to her human form. She looks very small without her wings. She takes a deep breath and puts a hand on Garmond's back, then looks at Kemnay and says to him, "Know, man, that I will do whatever I must to repair the wrongs here and I will accept any punishment it is mine to have." She then smiles and adds, "You know our names, from Balgavney, I expect. Will you give us yours?" She reaches a hand across the gateway.

He takes her hand and walks across the gateway to stand beside her. "I am Kemnay and this is Clola. In our village we were known as Paddler and Little One -- these are the names that Garmond would recognise." The wolf nods.

"I greet you, Kemnay and Clola. I am ready to do what I can," the young woman says, though her voice is hesitant. "However, in truth, I don't know what to do. Do you?" She looks up at Kemnay hopefully.

Kemnay shakes his head. "I know some of what we need, but I expect we will need Balgavney's help. Let's go up the hill and talk to her. I know she waits there." He picks up the basket and scattered pumpkins and together the four walk up the hill.

The man asks Fintray as they walk up the fields, "Can you drop the magical barrier so we can cross the hill? I have a camp below, but I expect we might be more comfortable in the village."

Fintray stops for a moment and closes her eyes, then shakes her head sadly. "No, I can't. It has something to do with the stones. I think I have to restore them before I will be allowed to do that."

Kemnay shrugs, as it is not unexpected. "Well, we shall ask if she has extra blankets that you can use and you can share our camp," he says with a calm smile.

As the four of them approach the top of the hill, the children notice them and run over. Ythsie throws herself into Fintray's arms. "Wolf Lady Angel!" the child says excitedly. "I knew you'd come. I've left flowers for you all the time. You are so beautiful, but where are your wings?" The child's voice is rapid and delighted. She releases Fintray, then runs over and hugs the wolf as well. Fintray and Garmond are astonished and they exchange a relieved look.

At the top of the hill Balgavney stands and looks at them. There are tears on her face, but she is smiling. Her voice is loving when she says, "Hello, Fintray, child. How glad I am to see you at last."

Fintray walks towards Balgavney and stops. "Balgavney, forgive me. I am so sorry. I did not mean to cause so much hurt." Tears wash down her young face.

"Oh, child," the wise woman says, "it was not intentional. You were frightened. I have come every day, watching for you, hoping you would hear me. I am so glad Kemnay was able to bring you back to us. Hello, Garmond, thank you for watching over her." There is true joy in her face. The loving power of forgiveness shines from the wise woman and wraps around all near her.

Fintray walks up to her friend and is enfolded in the wise woman's hug. Kemnay tries to join them but is stopped again by the magic.

Balgavney notices him stopped and says, "It seems your task is not done, my friend. I think Fintray must come with me to the village tonight and talk to everyone. I am sure once she realises that she is not held in anger, she will rest easy."

Kemnay accepts this and nods. He has to find Achath and expects he needs to be alone to do that. He says, "Fintray, I need you to come with me first, before you go to the village. We need to move the last stones to the circle, so they are safe and then I need to read them."

A look of pain crosses Balgavney's face, she says, "Must you disturb them? Can't they just be left to rest?" She is thinking of her daughter and her friends.

Clola says, "Balgavney, there is one here that doesn't belong. We have to find her. The only way we can do that is to speak to the stones. We will be as gentle as we can," the dragon promises.

Balgavney nods with understanding, then steps back and takes Fintray by the shoulders and says firmly, "Fintray, child, you may come to my home tonight and I will wait here to walk with you, but first you must take your family to the circle and let Kemnay speak with them."

The young woman's face is pained, but calm. The wise woman continues, "Tonight we will speak with the elders, and Pitsligo and Duffus so that we can know what needs to be done next." She turns Fintray back towards Kemnay and gives her a slight push to get her moving in his direction.

The wise woman calls out to the children, "Children, it is time to go back to the village. Skene, can you bring your mother's basket, please?" The children come running, and she hugs each one, then sends them off.

"I will wait for you here, for as long as it takes," Balgavney says gently as she settles again with her knitting.

Kemnay is humbled by Balgavney's calm and her love as well. He would not have been surprised to have anger directed at Fintray, but instead there is forgiveness. This wise woman is a great gift to her village.

Reading the stones

Together, Fintray, Garmond, Kemnay and Clola go down the hill to Rora Moss' home. They climb over the back fence and go into the house. There Fintray pauses, seeing the roof gone and much of the house in disrepair.

"It has been a very long time," she says sadly.

Garmond replies, "Yes, Wingling, it has. The only reason that the walls still stand is because the storms do not dance here. It is time to put it right, if we can."

The wolf walks over to the hearth where the two stones sit together. "Come, take up the man and the babe. She has not even seen a morning yet. It has been long enough."

Fintray walks over and carefully lifts the stones. For a moment she holds them to her heart and then she walks over to the kitchen hearth and looks at the stone there. She sways on her feet for a moment in memory of the terrible night. Kemnay puts a hand on her arm to steady her and she smiles weakly at him. In a swift motion she picks up the last stone and holds the three together. She walks to the back of the house and sees the wilting flowers by the small statue.

"Bless that child. I had only heard her voice before that night -- this is the first time I met her or her brother." Her hand reaches out and touch the flowers gently. "Thank you for your love and your trust." Tears fall like rain, but she is smiling.

"Come, Kemnay, it is time we put them all together again," the young woman says as she walks out of the house. Together they go down the hill to the village circle. Once inside Fintray puts the three stones she has with the others and asks the gods to allow Kemnay to speak with them and to keep them safe.

She walks out of the circle, with her hand resting on the head of the black wolf and turns back for a moment. "Again, I thank you. I promise to do what I can to help you find your friend." Fintray says quietly. "Now I must face those whom I have hurt so much." She and the wolf walk up the hill together towards the waiting wise woman.

Kemnay watches them walk away and then turns to his task. His hope is that he will find Achath among these souls, he suspects she is near. He sits on the ground in front of them, with Clola on his lap, and lifts them one at a time and speaks to them.

He leaves Rora Moss for last, as he wants first to identify the others so that he can make sure none are missing. He had forgotten to ask Balgavney how many last-life souls were lost that night. He finds Skirza and recognizes her because of her resemblance to her mother. He sends the thought that he is sorry to bother her, but she replies that she is not upset. Things need happen in their own time, and she will wait as long as needed. How like her mother she feels. He asks the names of all the last life souls and she tells him, so he knows he has them all.

After talking to all the stones, he finds they all have much the same message. There is no anger among them towards Fintray or Garmond, only patience and love. He finally picks up the stone that was Rora Moss. This one feels different to him and he realises this is a new soul, not a last-life one. It is innocent and untroubled. He feels that it is promised to the quiet lands, but doesn't understand how this can be. When he speaks to Rora Moss he finds out only her love and her memories. There is no sign of Achath here, and still there is a mystery. How can even the power of a wish stone have Rora Moss become a first life soul promised to the quiet lands?

He sets the stones together and leaves them safe in the circle. He feels he has found all of them, so tomorrow they will be ready to do what is needed with Fintray and Garmond. But what about Achath? Where is she?

He walks back to his camp at sunset with Clola on his shoulder. He is very tired and happily surprised to find a big basket from Tifty waiting by his fire. One of the children must have brought it down earlier. Together they make a good meal and again there is a pot of strong ale. The man relaxes by his fire and enjoys the ale while the dragon eats another pumpkin casserole. They settle comfortably to sleep.

Finding the wish stone

In the morning they meet Balgavney, Fintray and Garmond at the top of the hill.

Balgavney says to Kemnay, "We have figured out what needs to be done and how it can happen, but you must be included. We must find the wish stone Garmond hid and the stones of your parents must be brought as well." Kemnay looked stricken.

"But why would they matter here?" the man asks the wise woman.

She says to him quietly, "Because your grief and panic caused that. The price for you to settle things here is to face your own actions."

He says, brokenly, "But they are safe. Can they not be left to rest? It is miles from here, many seasons journey, and it will take me a very long time to get them and then return." His heart is heavy.

"No, because we have another way to bring them," Balgavney reassures him. "If Fintray shifts to her wings and combines her magic with Clola, they can be there and back in three days. Fintray can provide direction and protection, and Clola can carry them safely. In the meantime, you and Garmond can locate and recover the wish stone and we can be ready by sunrise on the fourth day."

Before Kemnay agrees, he asks, "What will happen to them? My father was dying, and my mother did not want to be without him. I do not want her returned to life to see him die again."

Fintray walks up to him and says, "They will wake for only an instant and then they will go to the quiet lands together. I promise you they will not suffer, in that moment."

He looks down at her and asks, "Can I tell them good bye? Without hurting them in any way?"

"Yes, but it will be only a short moment," Fintray warns.

"Thank you, Fintray, and you, Balgavney. Clola, you have heard what is needed. Off with you now," he says, hugging the small dragon just before she shifts to her great white flying form. Fintray shifts to her angel form and together they take off into the sky and are soon lost to sight.

Kemnay feels a bit lost, as he has never been separated from Clola before. Garmond looks after the flyers until they are long gone, and the sad set of his shoulders shows his feelings to be the same.

Kemnay walks over to Garmond and touches him gently. "Three days is not long. Where is the wish stone?" the man asks. "I believe that is where Achath is being held. We must find it."

"Under the stone holding the statue, buried in the ground," the wolf answers. "We must take down the statue, move the great base stone and dig it up." He says this matter-of-factly.

Kemnay groans and asks if any of the men from the village can help. There is no way he can move it alone.

Garmond walks down with him to look at it. "The statue is magical, so we should be able to remove it with magic. It is the base stone that is the problem. Possibly with ropes and oxen we might pull it out of the way."

As the two approach the statue, they find it is gone and only the large stone remains.

"Just as I thought," Garmond says. "Once she left, the image of that statue was broken. It was just a reflection of our hidden form, out in plain sight so it would not be found. The others I watch, so they remain. She controls the melding, which is why I could not escape her. The others are just copies made of actual rock."

Kemnay takes a look at the pedestal and then returns to ask Balgavney to find someone with a team and ropes to help.

Even with the help of all of the men of the village it takes the full three days to move the stone, as much digging has to be done around it as well. One it is moved enough, Garmond digs out the wish stone and takes it in his mouth. He tries to give it to Kemnay to read, but it will not let him touch it.

At sunset Fintray and Clola return, both of them tired and hungry. Clola sets the joined stones of his parents in his hand and he once again feels their love. How he has missed them. He takes this stone and puts it safely with the others from the village. Now that all have been gathered and the wish stone found, in the morning they will be able to repair what has happened.

That night, Kemnay bathes in the river and plays with Clola. He has missed her, mischief and all. He has two full pumpkins baked and waiting for her, which she happily gorges herself on. He asks about the journey and the village.

Clola says, "It was interesting to fly with a human person, but I missed the boat. It is very fast to fly with combined magic, but not as interesting. The village is well and thriving. Merry has gone on to her next rebirth many seasons past, so you had no need to worry. The current wise woman was glad to know these souls would be sent on. She sends you her blessings."

All are removed from suffering

Just before dawn, Fintray and Garmond come into their camp. Together, the four of them go to the village circle. Kemnay takes the stone of his parents, Garmond takes the wish stone, and Fintray carries the others in the magical bag. Clola leads the way up the hill to where all of the villagers wait.

At the front of the crowd stands Balgavney, still on the other side of the barrier. She gives quiet instructions to everyone.

Kemnay reads each stone and calls out its name. A member of the soul's family comes to collects the stone, moved by a child. Then they begin to form a circle. Each stone is held between two hands of family or friends. A chain of love, with each stone held between two living hands.

Balgavney takes Skirza's stone and holds it with Tifty, who holds the stone of her father Strathy in her other hand. Skene holds Strathy as well, and in his other hand is the baby Cullerlie. Ythsie holds her too and in her other hand is the stone of Rora Moss, which will also be held with Fintray's hand.

Fintray will stand in the barrier and complete the link, holding Kemnay's hand with his parents between them. One of the other children is on the other side of Kemnay, just holding his hand. Before Fintray takes Kemnay's hand, she tells Garmond to put the wish stone in the centre of the circle and to stand with her. They will invoke it one last time together. Clola was sitting in her usual place on Kemnay's left shoulder.

As the sun touches the hill tops, Fintray closes the circle. She melds with Garmond and they shifts to the great form of the Wolf Angel and in a loud voice she says, "In the name of all the gods of the earth, sea and sky, I invoke this wish stone to undo a terrible wrong. Hear me and attend."

Suddenly all the stones are restored and there is much hugging and rejoicing happening. Kemnay turns to see his parents there and Fintray standing behind them. She whispers, "Hurry, there isn't long."

Kemnay hugs his parents to his chest and says, "I love you. Please forgive me."

His father laughs and says, "Thank you, son. You have granted what we wished. I love you."

His mother says happily, "Of course we forgive you, and I love you too."

Then in an instant they were gone. Fintray looks at him and says, "I held them as long as I could. They are now in the quiet lands, well and happy together always."

Kemnay's tears fell quietly. "Thank you, Fintray, I know you did your best. Now go greet your family."

He looks off to the sea, not realising that the barrier around him has dropped and he is surrounded by happy people. His heart is so sad.

Then from he feels a small hand pulling on him from behind, and he looks down and sees Ythsie's happy face.

The child says to him, "I found your friend, see?" She is holding the hand of Achath. Clola launches herself at the woman and is soon being hugged, but all the while the wise woman's eyes hold the man's as he stands in shock.

He can only stare at her as she stands smiling at him. His mouth works but he has no voice. "Achath?" he tries to say. Suddenly his knees go weak and he falls to the ground. She comes over to him and kneels down beside him, putting a soft hand on his neck.

"Yes, I am real, you are not dreaming. I was hidden in the wish stone. The gods required my soul to be held to make the trade of a new soul instead of mine, but I was trapped until you could find me and set me free," she says cheerfully.

Clola dances around the two of them on the ground. Kemnay puts up a hand to touch Achath's face. "I never stopped looking for you," he says, his voice gruff with tears.

"I know that," she says, smiling at him.

"I love you, Achath," he whispers to her, afraid of what she might say.

"I know that too. It certainly took you long enough to figure it out." Achath says, laughing as she leans down and kisses him softly on the lips.

The End

Made in the USA
Lexington, KY
04 August 2010